SOUTH
CAROLINA
HAUNTS

KEVIN THOMAS WARD

**Other Schiffer Books
on Related Subjects:**

Arizona's Haunted Hotspots,
978-0-7643-3748-2, $16.99

Florida's Haunted Hospitality,
978-0-7643-4120-5, $16.99

Haunted Theaters of the Carolinas,
978-0-7643-3327-9, $14.99

UFOs Over South Carolina,
978-0-7643-4749-8, $16.99

Designed by Brenda McCallum
Cover design by Matt Goodman
Type set in Nightmare5/Times
ISBN: 978-0-7643-4770-2
Printed in The United States of America

Published by Schiffer Publishing, Ltd.
4880 Lower Valley Road
Atglen, PA 19310
Phone: (610) 593-1777;
Fax: (610) 593-2002
E-mail: Info@schifferbooks.com

For our complete selection of fine books
on this and related subjects, please visit our
website at www.schifferbooks.com. You
may also write for a free catalog.

This book may be purchased from the
publisher. Please try your bookstore first.

We are always looking for people to write
books on new and related subjects. If you
have an idea for a book, please contact us
at proposals@schifferbooks.com.

Schiffer Publishing's titles are available at
special discounts for bulk purchases for sales
promotions or premiums. Special editions,
including personalized covers, corporate
imprints, and excerpts can be created in
large quantities for special needs. For more
information, contact the publisher.

DEDICATION

To my father Rodney Darnay Ward ...
No one could ask for a better father

Acknowledgments

This book would not have been possible without the help and support of so many. First, I would like to thank my friend and editor, Steven Smith: You have been a huge help. To my sister, Lisa Meadows: You have always been an inspiration to and sounding board for me. The fine folks of South Carolina who have helped me complete this project, and the very helpful folks at the Old City Jail and the Pelican to name but two who were of great help!

ANTIGONISH

Yesterday, upon the stair,
I met a man who wasn't there
He wasn't there again today
I wish, I WThe Lady in Bluee'd go away...

When I came home last night at three
The man was waiting there for me
But when I looked around the hall
I couldn't see him there at all!
Go away, go away, don't you come back any more!
Go away, go away, and please don't slam the door...

Last night I saw upon the stair
A little man who wasn't there
He wasn't there again today
Oh, how I wish he'd go away

~ Hughes Mearns, Educator and poet

CONTENTS

INTRODUCTION

For the last six years, my friend Chris and I have taken a trip to Florida. Along the way, we stop in Charleston, South Carolina, one of the loveliest cities I have ever been to, which is why we stop there every year. I look forward to going there every time ... I find myself enthralled by the city's amazing history. When you visit Charleston, it is like stepping through a doorway into the past; monuments and historic buildings seem to be everywhere! To history nuts like me, this offers such breathtaking appeal.

Four years ago, on one of our annual visits, we decided to take a ghost tour. While I am a huge paranormal enthusiast, Chris only "entertains" interest. Nevertheless, we decided to remedy the fact we had never taken a ghost tour before. Deciding which tour to take was not easy, as Charleston boasts many available options that cover one end of the city to the other. Ultimately, I felt drawn to the one for the Old City Jail ... if only because the building looks like something from a horror film, which compelled me to take this particular tour.

The tour was well done by our guide. Not only did it provide ghost stories we had expected, but it also gave a comprehensive history of the troubled building. Combined with the building's overall creepiness, this made for a good time for anyone who likes a good ghost story. Sadly, despite taking tons of pictures — some through an infrared lens — I never saw a single specter during the tour (this did not diminish my enjoyment). Later on, I read about Charleston's other haunted locations, which inevitably led me to investigate the rest of the state. Every town has its own collection of haunted locations. During this investigatory period, I was in the process of finishing my debut book, *North Carolina Haunts*. As I went through my research, I began to realize that once I completed compiling paranormal tales of my home state, I wanted to write about South Carolina's ghost stories.

Even as I was adding the finishing touches to my other book, I began researching locations for this book, reading about more famous ghosts, such as the Gray Man, as well as less-renowned specters like the one at "Snow House." I found the people of South Carolina to be so kind and more than willing to help as I did interviews; they seemed go out of their way to be of assistance, sharing old stories or personal encounters. Though the experiences were delightful, this book only contains a small fraction of South Carolina's ghosts, but rest assured — they are among the best the state has to offer!

Before we get into the crux of the book, it would help to have some of the state's history.

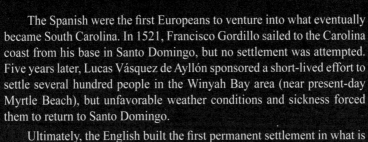

The Spanish were the first Europeans to venture into what eventually became South Carolina. In 1521, Francisco Gordillo sailed to the Carolina coast from his base in Santo Domingo, but no settlement was attempted. Five years later, Lucas Vásquez de Ayllón sponsored a short-lived effort to settle several hundred people in the Winyah Bay area (near present-day Myrtle Beach), but unfavorable weather conditions and sickness forced them to return to Santo Domingo.

Ultimately, the English built the first permanent settlement in what is modern-day Charleston. During 1663, the English colonized the province known as Carolina, named for England's current monarch, Charles the 1st. In the beginning, the colony was simply Carolina, but in 1712, it split into two regions. By 1719, South Carolina was officially born.

Decades later South Carolina played a crucial part in the American Revolution, having more battles fought on her lands than any other colony. In battlefields like Kings Mountain and Camden, brave men laid down their lives for the cause of freedom. It is said that some of those men can still be heard carrying on the fight to this day. On May 23, 1788, South Carolina became the eighth state to join the Union when it signed off on the U.S. Constitution.

As of 1860, South Carolina was one of the wealthiest states, mostly due to its ports and the massive number of plantations. As most people are aware, the state was the first to secede during the time leading up to the American Civil War.

There were so many young lives were lost in those few years during a war where brother fought brother. The entire state has many well-preserved pieces of history: old homes, battlefields, and cemeteries. Because of this, it is possible that the dead will trick themselves into believing they are still alive and refuse to depart this world. So now, without further ado, let us begin our journey into haunted South Carolina.

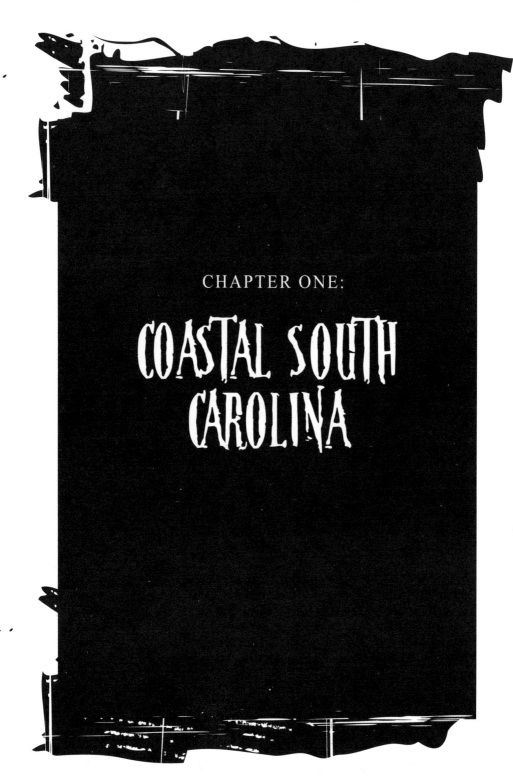

CHAPTER ONE:

COASTAL SOUTH CAROLINA

The Lady in Blue

THE BLUE LADY

HILTON HEAD
SOUTH CAROLINA

The Blue Lady is known throughout the entire state. She is a specter seen in the Hilton Head area. She has made regular appearances for over a century in the Palmetto Dunes vicinity.

It seems every area has a famous, wandering female ghost. In my home state of North Carolina, the Pink Lady is known in the mountains. It is fitting, then, that South Carolina would have the Blue Lady of the Coast. Female ghost stories share a common element: the women normally suffer a tragedy so traumatizing, it keeps them from leaving this earthly plane. It is possible that these women do not want to leave, but perhaps some of them do not realize they have passed on.

Differences do exist, though, among the Blue and Pink Lady stories. The Pink Lady is said to have taken her life after her fiancé cheated on her. On the other hand, the Blue Lady has a more touching story. There are a few different versions of the Blue Lady's tragic tale, but they share certain facts.

Her name was Caroline Fripp, daughter of Adam Fripp, the lighthouse keeper. By 1898, he had been the caretaker for three years and had done his duty with pride. He was tasked with keeping the light burning during the night. Knowing that the simple light could mean the very difference between life and death for a ship and her crew, he knew the importance of his job. His daughter, Caroline, had become his apprentice and helped him in various ways, including polishing the lens of the lighthouse. Their seclusion brought Caroline very close to her father, and in many ways she became his entire world. August came, and the little island had survived without a single hit, but by the 30th of that month, Adam Fripp knew their luck had run out — a hurricane, which formed near Florida, was making its way up the coast and the Fripps' little island sat in its warpath. Adam locked himself inside the lighthouse, knowing that no matter what, the light must stay lit. In that perilous time, every ship was counting on him.

Finding shore at night is hard enough; add a hurricane into the mix and clear sight is more or less impossible. Despite her father's insistence to stay in the home, Caroline joined him in the lighthouse to perform his duties. In the early part of the storm, they noticed a small ship off the shore. The ruthless hurricane tossed around the tiny vessel like a leaf in the wind. As the storm worsened, the Fripps' task became even harder. First, the winds smashed the windows open. Soon after, the hurricane blew out the light. Adam was ready to reignite it, even though the wind would blow it back out only a few minutes later.

Regardless, he relit it every time. Anyone who has attempted to light a match on a windy day knows how frustrating it is to ignite, as, mere seconds later, it extinguishes. Imagine the anguish Adam, who had whole ships full of lives depending on him, must have felt. Soon after, Caroline attempted to return to the house and find something that could block the shattered windows. However, when she reached the bottom of the stairs, she found it flooded. The ever-rising ocean now covered the entire island. Caroline and Adam were stranded in the lighthouse, and the water was climbing higher every minute as the night went on. Despite all this, the Fripps kept the light burning until the storm passed. This should have been reason enough to celebrate, but, sadly, the stress of the night took a tragic toll on Adam and he suffered a heart attack during the night.

Even though the island was partially flooded, Caroline got her father to their house and into bed. Meanwhile, water sloshed about them. Adam suffered a few hours before finally breathing his last and leaving this world behind. In losing her father, Caroline became an emotional wreck: she not only lost her father, but also her closet friend. She felt alone and adrift in the world. Legends say that she refused to accept her father's death. She continued to wear the blue dress she had on when he died and began walking the beach every night in a daze, staring out to sea. Eventually, she, too, passed away (though according to some versions, she died in the hurricane like her father). Soon after her passing, reports came in of her ethereal form walking the same shore she did in life.

Not unlike the Gray Man of Pawleys Island, the Blue Lady normally appears right before a hurricane strikes the island, although she does not offer protection to those who see her. Still, she is not described as a frightful spirit. In fact, most people never get a clear look at her face, yet it is not uncommon for amateur paranormal investigators and young people looking for unique activities, to travel to the Blue Lady's stomping grounds, hoping to a catch a glimpse of the somber girl.

Often, visitors only succeed in scaring themselves; the blowing wind becomes unearthly whispers, the moonlight shining down becomes ghosts. It seems the Blue Lady very seldom makes an appearance when people are attempting to see her. More often than not, the people not looking for earthbound souls end up seeing her. Maybe she dislikes being a mere attraction to people; after all, by every account of her story, she walks this stretch of land because of the tragedy that befell her one horrible day. To make light of her sorrow would burden even a ghost's heart.

The Pirate Ghost protects his captain's treasure.

GHOST TREASURE OF FOLLY ISLAND

FOLLY ISLAND
SOUTH CAROLINA

This story involves one of everyone's favorite premises: buried treasure, the notion of riches beyond measure resting under only a few feet of sand. When I went to the beach as a young boy, I would take my plastic shovel and dig like crazy in hopes of finding the classic wooden chest full of gold coins. I never did find it, though, and very seldom does anyone else. There are exceptions, though. Once, at a fifty-year veteran's reunion for the Civil War, a man known as Yokum shared a story with his fellow brothers in arms.

Civil War combat only touched Folly Island on May 10, 1863, when Confederate forces attacked Federal forces. As the Union army prepared for an attack on the important port of Charleston, they knew they needed to seize Folly Island. The island fell after a very brief battle. Members of the Union scoured the island to gather the few people who lived there and transport them off the island. The move ensured that islanders would not learn anything of the Union's plans, which could reach the Confederacy. A young officer named Yokum was assigned to help with the evacuation. He was nearing the end of his task when he noticed one last run-down shack in the distance. After knocking on the door, he was greeted by an elderly black woman with a child. Yokum informed her she had to leave the island for an uncertain amount of time. The woman protested, having nowhere else to go. Instead of leaving, she began telling stories of her life in the house. At this point, Yokum was already tired from walking the island, but decided to at least pretend to listen. Her tale was going in one ear and out the other, until she mentioned a bit about pirates and buried treasure. This, of course, would catch anyone's attention.

She told Yokum that a group of pirates had come ashore when she was a young girl. The buccaneers dug a hole between two big oaks and lowered six chests of gold, silver, and jewels into it. When the last chest was in place, the captain stabbed one of his crew in the back and threw his body in the hole. The gang then covered the hole and sailed away, never to return. His interest piqued, Yokum wanted more information and he asked the woman why she did not dig up the gold herself. Her response: Only a fool would dig it up. She explained that the captain did not kill the man simply out of malice. In death, the pirate's cursed soul would guard the captain's treasure; at least, this was the intention. Yokum laughed at such a thought and then helped the woman and her child onto a nearby boat.

Later that night, once camp had been made, Yokum decided to share the pirate story with his friend Hatcher, who at first doubted the tale. Yokum admitted he doubted the story, as well, but reminded him that they were the only two on the island who knew of it. He also mentioned that after leaving, they may never be able to return and confirm the story as true. Eventually, they agreed to search for the treasure. They found the two oak trees and started digging.

Oddly, the further they got, the more the wind seemed to pick up. Soon, the trees were swayed as if caught in a storm, yet nothing else seemed affected by the mysterious gale. Still, the men continued to dig, driven by the delicious thought of striking gold. Suddenly, bizarre lights appeared in the sky. At first, Yokum and Hatcher suspected lightning, but not a single cloud floated in the sky. Soon the lights brightened and began moving quickly. From the cluster of lights emerged a black, shadowy figure. Initially, the men thought maybe a fellow solider, curious about their digging, was approaching them, but then Hatcher noted the figure was dressed in pirate's clothing and carried a large sword. Frightened out of their wits, both men dropped their shovels and made a run back to their camp. When they arrived, they hid in their tent and kept an eye out till morning. Both men, knowing they would sound crazy to their brothers-in-arms, decided to never share their story.

By the time the fifty-year reunion took place, Hatcher was dead and Yokum, aware that his time was short, no longer cared if people called him crazy. He now shared his tale with anyone who would listen. Surprisingly, the men in attendance received his story fairly well, but then again, the veterans merely assumed Yokum was sharing a tall tale. Yokum insisted, with every ounce of his being, that his story was completely true. The story would have most likely died with Yokum, had it not been for a man named Frances Moore. Frances, who was attending the event, was so enthralled by the ghostly tale, he wrote it down and had it published in the paper. The story has survived ever since.

The gold, if it ever existed, has never been found. Because many powerful hurricanes have hit the island over the century, Folly's twin oaks are surely long gone. So, if you ever decide to look for the pirates' loot forgotten by history, be prepared to dig for your life! And if strong winds crash over you as your shovel tears into the ground, while odd lights appear above, know that you are close to your treasure. However, unless you want to meet the wraith of the tormented soul left to guard the chest, I suggest you learn from Yokum and make a run for it!

The Attack on Fort Wagner.

THE GHOST OF FORT WAGNER

FOLLY BEACH
SOUTH CAROLINA

I have been to a number of Civil War sites in my three decades, and each comes with its own story. Some tales are bloodier than others while some still hold more significance to the war's conclusion. Regardless of their differences, all the stories are important because of the lives lost in fighting them.

Fort Wagner, located on Morris Island, was built to protect the southern approach to Charleston during the Civil War. It was the best beach defense devised by the Confederate Army, and it withstood multiple assaults from Union forces.

The First Battle of Fort Wagner occurred on July 11, 1863. Fort Wagner was a simple fort of earth, sand, and some lumber. Yet, during the battle, only twelve

Confederate soldiers died. This is a startling comparison to the Union's 339 losses. However, the Union would not be deterred so easily and they planned another attack.

The Second Battle of Fort Wagner occurred a week later, on July 18th. This Union attack is well remembered for those who led it, the 54th Massachusetts Volunteer infantry, comprised of black soldiers led by Colonel Gould Shaw. Despite The 54th's defeat and many casualties (including Colonel Shaw), they are remembered as the first non-white troops given an important offensive. Although a tactical defeat, the Second Battle of Fort Wagner provided action for black troops in the Civil War and spurred additional recruitment of black volunteers.

The Massachusetts 24th attempted to take the Fort on August 25th, but their attack would also fail. Another siege took place the next day, and finally, on September 6th, the Confederate army abandoned the fort. Not all of the credit belongs to the brave men of the 24th; other recognition certainly belongs to the men who died trying to take the fort during the previous attempts.

After each attack, the men stationed at Wagner would bury the bodies of their fallen enemies in quickly-dug graves around the Fort. These graves would eventually be part of the Confederate soldiers' undoing. With so many dead bodies decomposing near the Fort, the freshwater supply quickly became polluted. From a morbid perspective, the men who died trying to take the Fort did, in death, actually complete their mission.

The simple earthwork Fort has long-ago been washed away by the ever-encroaching sea. Although the Fort itself is long gone, it is not forgotten. Wagner exists in countless books, and has been featured in the major motion picture *Glory*. In modern days, however, most folks in the Folly Beach area have little concern over the fate of the Fort. Instead, their interest lies in the souls of those who died in the multiple attempts to take it.

Now, I should make this clear: Not everyone is positive the ghosts of Folly Beach are those of Civil War soldiers, at least not all of them. Even reports from the 1880s speak of odd occurrences on the beach. One story tells of a man walking the beach in the early 1900s. It was around dusk, and he was heading away from the shore when he saw what looked like three approaching men. As they neared him, the man noticed a lack of facial features on the three strangers — their faces seemed to be pitch-black. When the man backed up in fear, the three figures simply faded away. Wanting to be safe than sorry, he made a hasty exit from the vicinity. These shadow men are seen all over the beach. Normally, they do not stay around for long; the gentleman on the beach saw them longer than most people. It is more common to see them for less than five seconds. Some folks actually report seeing the full apparitions of Union soldiers walking the beach. The spectral troops stride steadily towards Fort Wagner, still conducting the siege, though the ocean has long since swallowed their target whole. The soldiers are also thought to be responsible for odd voices heard on the beach at night. People who find themselves near the shore after sunset claim to hear conversation buzzing around them. Unfortunately, they cannot make out what is being said, but most agree it is the sound of two or more men chatting away. Perhaps they are discussing the siege that they still think is raging on. Or maybe, just maybe, they are simply talking about their favorite fruit. Who knows?

Folks who walk the beach also claim to be overcome by powerful, out-of-place emotions. Fear or anger will consume one's heart even on a day of peace and relaxation. The feelings always come and go quickly, and create the experience of stepping into someone else's mind for a brief moment. Cold spots, common in all haunted locations, are also felt here. Folks strolling on the beach in the hot summer will find themselves walking through a wintry chill. A cool breeze on the beach is very common, but the temperatures people experience are definitely below cool.

Now, all of these phenomena are enough to get goose bumps on the skin and yet, the one I find most chilling is not one of sight or sound, but of smell. In the Civil War, when a limb was damaged in battle, the most common treatment was amputation. After all, medical science barely existed then. To many of the souls that fought in that bloody war, a military doctor's tent was more terrifying than any enemy fort. Because of the large number of wounded patients, doctors could only offer a shot of whiskey for the pain. Before a man could swallow, he had the saw cutting through him.

As the sieges continued, the number of wounded increased. This, of course, meant the removal of more arms and legs. The severed limbs had to be disposed of before they started to rot and possibly affect the health of the soldiers. The disposal was to burn them in huge bonfires. The smell of burning flesh, I hear, is mighty unpleasant. Luckily, I have never had to experience it. People in the area still smell the odor of burning human remains as it drifts across the shore. Ask anyone who has smelled the stench on the beach, and they will assure you there is no mistaking it. So if you ever find yourself on Folly Beach and you hear the sound of men talking when no one is around or you smell an unpleasant odor, maybe you should take a moment to pay your respects to those who died there.

An ethereal soldier and his horse.

THE GHOSTLY WEDDING

PAWLEYS ISLAND
SOUTH CAROLINA

I have been to a number of weddings in my time, and all of them are happy occasions. They are something we hope to remember for as long as we can: we film them, take pictures, and try to mentally catch every detail of the day. Now, almost no big day goes exactly as planned; in fact, one of the last I attended the DJ never showed up. It did upset the bride a bit, but they made the best of it and ended up enjoying their wedding day. Here is a story in which the big day did not go as planned and it would have been a lot harder to make the best of it.

The ghost story did not begin in the final days of the Civil War; rather, it took place fifty-three years *after* the war's final shots. It was a warm summer night at Hagley Landing. Eugene LaBruce was working a job, taxiing folks who came ashore at Hagley Landing to Pawleys Island. One night, LaBruce, as he waited for the next boat, stared off into the murky darkness. This was something he did frequently while waiting for his next fare.

On that particular night, something unusual occurred ... something he would never forget for as long as he lived. After a time, he noted that he was not alone. Quite the contrary, he seemed to be amidst a crowd of people. The curious thing about this was that only a moment before he had been alone on a dock in pitch-black darkness. Now, very unexpectedly, he stood next to people who did not acknowledge his presence. Everyone appeared to be celebrating, cheering and clapping, but it took him a few moments to discern why. Finally, LaBruce learned the reason.

It began with a love triangle between two friends smitten with the same woman — a story we have read in books and seen played out in the movies and on television a hundred times. One of them was believed to have died in a battlefield far away in the Civil War. After courting each other for a while, the lady married the other suitor, who thought with his friend gone the issue was settled. The newly-married couple exited a church and the gathered people erupted with clapping. A commotion suddenly arose nearby and a man, dressed in Confederate uniform, rode up on horseback. He demanded they stop the wedding because he was this woman's true love and could not bear to see her marry any other man, even his best friend. To the young soldier's dismay, he learned that he arrived too late — they had married only minutes beforehand. His love, the new bride, informed the solider she had not heard from him in three years and was sure he had perished in a battle, so she had to move on. The solider dismounted and came face-to-face with his former friend, the man now married to his lost love. They were preparing to go to blows when the young bride, in anguish, ran towards the water in an apparent suicide attempt...

It was this post-wedding scene that played out before LaBruce now. Before the bride reached the water, though, a docking boat signaled and snapped LaBruce out of his reverie. The wedding guests and solider vanished ... It was as if they had never been there in the first place.

Not wishing to appear as if he had lost his marbles, LaBruce acted as if the previous minutes had passed uneventfully. Upon the arrival of a young, female passenger, he greeted her and proceeded onward, towards Pawleys Island. As they drove along a dark stretch of road, and despite the fact he could not rid his mind of the surreal, ghostly wedding, the taxi man engaged his passenger in small talk. Unexpectedly, in the murk ahead, two figures — the bride and her husband — appeared as tangible as they did on their wedding day, though their features were somber and unflinching, LaBruce quickly swerved to avoid a collision and nearly flipped in the process.

Turning to see if the people on the road were unhurt, he beheld an empty road and darkness. Breathing heavily and deeply shaken, LaBruce apologized and told his passenger he thought he had seen something, but it must have been his imagination. Quite unexpectedly, his passenger responded, "It wasn't your imagination. I saw them too!"

LaBruce would never discover the identity of the spectral couple or if the bride had, in fact, taken her own life. Regardless, the ghostly replay of that wedding day seems to indicate that, no matter what, there might be some unfinished business underfoot. No one has ever reported seeing this replayed, so maybe the specter or specters arranged for that one show to make sure their story would be told.

THE GRAY MAN

PAWLEYS ISLAND
SOUTH CAROLINA

South Carolina's most well-known specter resides on a little stretch of land called Pawleys Island. Locals simply call him the Gray Man. His reputation spreads throughout South Carolina and beyond: I grew up in North Carolina and remember hearing about him as a child. His appearance is a blessing and an omen; although he manifests right before a hurricane, those who see him seem to receive protection. Truthfully, he is more a guardian angel of Pawleys Island than he is a ghost.

There are several stories about the origin of this beloved specter, but the most popular concerns two young lovers separated by death in 1822.

A young planter returning from a long absence was eager to see his fiancée, even though the wedding was only days away. Accompanied by his manservant on horseback, he rode from Georgetown for his love's family home at Pawleys Island. The planter was so eager to see his precious fiancée that he decided not to follow the road. Instead, he took a shortcut across the marsh. This route was dangerous and his horse, moving at full speed, stumbled through quicksand. Both the horse and rider perished when they slammed into the ground. The planter's fiancée learned of his death shortly after. She fell into such a deep depression that she started wandering the beach to overcome her loss. One windy summer day, she saw a gray, smoky figure on the beach. As she approached him, she recognized her lover's face, but before she could get closer, he disappeared. Later that night, he visited her in her dream, appearing as he did in life. The only words he offered were, "Leave the island, the wind is coming." After the young woman told her parents of her dream, they fled to the mainland. That night, a hurricane crashed ashore, destroying nearly every home on the island. The young woman's home was left untouched by the storm, as though an unseen force had protected it.

Decades would pass before another recorded sighting of the Gray Man took place. In August of 1893, the Gray Man appeared to a farmer from the Lachicotte family who was herding animals off the island. The other islanders noticed the coming storm and were trying to prepare. The Lachicotte farmer found a young

The earliest known photo of The Gray Man.

man dressed in gray standing by a tree. He motioned for the quiet lad to follow him off the island for his safety. However, the Gray Man just stood there silently. The farmer, not wanting to ask again, kept on his way, assuming that the boy was simply crazy. The hurricane, called the Sea Islands Hurricane, killed an estimated 1,500 people, yet not only did the farmer's home survive, but it also was virtually untouched.

The Gray Man showed up again on October 15, 1954. Bill Collins was honeymooning with his new bride on Pawleys Island. At 5 a.m., Bill woke up to a persistent knock on his door. Aware that no good news comes at that hour, he anxiously rushed to answer the door. A young man dressed in gray stood on his doorstep; a large, brimmed hat covered the features of his face. He told Bill the Red Cross sent him to warn of a storm and he needed to evacuate the island. The young man then turned and walked down the stairs. Bill stuck his head out to ask how much time remained, but the gray-clad visitor had simply vanished. Shortly after, Bill realized that the man's clothing seemed to echo another time and smelled of ocean water. Despite this, he woke up his new bride and immediately got off the island. When they returned, the island's beachfront property was a mere dump — the storm had wiped out almost everyone's home. However, Bill's house stood unharmed. In fact, the beach towels still hung on the railing as they did the day before. Anyone would have to assume that something or someone had shielded the home from the storm entirely.

The Gray Man once again made his presence known on September 19, 1989. Pawleys Island residents Clara and Jack Moore were walking the beach and simply enjoying each other's company as they usually did. They were used to seeing people on the beach with them, but that day they saw only one other person. A young man was enjoying a peaceful stroll in the ocean air. Although Jack had never seen this man before, his Southern hospitality dictated he say a friendly greeting on passing someone, so, as he got closer, he began to speak … but the young man had vanished entirely. Naturally, there is nowhere to hide on a long stretch of beach, so the stranger's departure was a true mystery. Still, Jack and Clara did not worry too much about the strange happening and put it in the back of their minds. Soon they received word that Hurricane Hugo was going to make landfall, so they packed and left for the mainland.

On September 22nd, Hugo hit South Carolina, destroying over 9,000 homes. When Bill and Clara finally returned to the island, they found that their home had been undamaged by Hugo. Unfortunately, many others were gone. They did not realize why their home remained intact until they read an article in the local paper. According to the article, the Gray Man failed to appear this time. Clara then realized the man they saw on the beach was, in fact, the fabled spirit and credited him with saving their home.

The old plantation.

LITCHFIELD PLANTATION

PAWLEYS ISLAND
SOUTH CAROLINA

There is a beautiful bed and breakfast at the Litchfield Plantation, which is located on Pawleys Island. As with our theme, this is no ordinary bed and breakfast, since it comes with its very own spook-in-residence!

A man, Peter Simon, originally built the house around 1740 after having recently purchased the land. He died in 1794, having lived there for more than fifty years, leaving three sons and large amounts of land behind. In his will, Simon stipulated that the land was to be divided up between his sons. His son, John Simon, got Litchfield, but did not seem keen on keeping it. This was evident in 1796 when he sold it to Daniel Tucker.

Litchfield seemed to bounce from one owner to another. In 1797, John Tucker inherited Litchfield from his father, Daniel. In 1859, after John Tucker's death,

Litchfield passed to his son, Dr. Henry Massingberd Tucker, said to be the most famous of the former owners. Famous or not, he only lived there a brief time before he left to join the Confederate Army in 1860. After the end of the war, however, he returned home to Litchfield, which he sold in 1897 to a man named Louis Claude Lachicotte. The house would go through several more owners before finally coming into the hands of the Litchfield Plantation Company in 1969, which still currently owns it. They have done quite a bit with the former plantation to transform it into a must-see for tourists on the island. Among the transformations was the converting of the house into a bed and breakfast.

Some of the folks that have visited the old home whisper that it is haunted by its former owner, Henry Tucker. This is somewhat puzzling, to a certain extent, because he barely lived there long enough, at least as its owner. Granted, I'm sure he spent a good bit of time on this property, especially when his father owned it, so it makes sense that he would be attached to the plantation.

Back when Dr. Henry Tucker lived at the plantation, he doubtlessly spent much of his free time making house calls to his patients on the island. The family employed an old native as gatekeeper to the island. The man's only job was to open the gate when welcoming guests or residents of the home returned. It is said that this job failed to hold his interest and he often wandered off.

Henry normally returned home later in the evening. A bell on the outside of the gate rang when people wanted to summon the old gatekeeper. However, for the doctor, it never seemed to work. As a result, he would grow impatient and start ringing it as violently and loudly as possible. Still, it seemed the bell was out of the old man's hearing range and he would often have to let himself in. First, he would tie his horse on the outside of the gate and use it as a sort of step stool to crawl over the wall. Finally, once he got across the wall, he and his horse would make their way to the house. Because of the late hour, Henry would not use the main stairs to his room, but a small set of stairs used by the servants.

There is no telling how many times Henry did this, or for that matter, how the gatekeeper kept his job! Eventually, the doctor probably grew accustomed to this frustrating routine. Even in death, though, he is reportedly still performing his wall-climbing act. Not long after he left this mortal coil, owners of the property would awaken, at ungodly hours, to the sound of bells at the gate. Each time an incident was inspected, no one would be found at the gate. Everyone's first thought, of course, was that some local kids or drunkard was having some fun at their expense. Yet, almost in response to this, the next time it rang, the ringing persisted until someone reached the gate. When that person got there, they witnessed the bell ringing, even though no one was pulling the string. Finally, after years of these bizarre occurrences, the owner removed the bell because he no longer had the patience to entertain the ghost. Despite this, the ringing is still heard now and again. The bell's removal has only accomplished two things: it is now twice as creepy and no one bothers to see who is there anymore.

Another sound nearby is that of a horse clopping around the outside of the gate. It is most likely Henry's horse, of course. More than one former gatekeeper has heard the sound of an approaching horse. Naturally, the gatekeeper would prepare to greet the rider, but the horse never arrived.

The doctor is not just heard, but is actually seen. Imagine the alarm if you saw a man walking across your front lawn and making his way towards your house at 2 a.m.! Many people have experienced this sighting — they see the stranger avoid the main entrance and make his way to the servants' stairs. Any man who witnessed this would dash towards the entrance by the stairs, expecting to catch the would-be intruder. Instead, they find the door completely locked, with no signs of forced entry. After walking one end of the house to another, the gatekeeper would finally accept that no one got in...at least, no one living.

The phantom intruder is still seen to this day and is considered to be none other than Dr. Tucker finally making it home. Once he has entered the home, he never causes any mischief. There are no reports of odd encounters with Tucker within the walls of the plantation. I personally think the good doctor is a "residual haunting"; he is unaware of all the changes to his former home or who lives there. In other words, he is like a looped scene in a movie, reliving one of the nights he had to let himself in and, once he has accomplished his task, he starts it right back over.

So if you ever find yourself at the Litchfield Plantation and hear a bell ringing or see a man walking towards the house, just smile and nod at Dr. Tucker and welcome him home!

The Pelican Inn.

THE PELICAN INN

PAWLEYS ISLAND
SOUTH CAROLINA

Pawleys Island is home to the beautiful Pelican Inn, known for its breathtaking setting and its simple elegance. Though modernized, the Inn was not originally built for the purpose it now serves. It once was a simple home. What's more, it is one of the very few original homes left on Pawleys Island. The Inn's current owner, Corinne Taylor, was more than happy to fill me in on all the history of the home.

The Inn was constructed by a man named Plowden Charles Jenrette Weston of Hagley Plantation in 1858. At that point, malaria season was approaching, so it was not uncommon for well-off people to avoid heavily populated areas, where malaria would be widespread. Because Pawleys Island was very scarcely populated, Weston deemed it the perfect place. His home, like most on the island, was constructed with cypress lumber. Obviously lacking our modern air-conditioning, its doors and windows were designed to maximize ventilation. As a result, the ocean breeze became natural. Sadly, he passed away from tuberculosis shortly after moving in. As a result, his home came to have a new owner.

As mentioned earlier, the Pelican Inn is one of the few original homes left. However, mere luck alone has not spared it from destruction. Due to Weston's wise judgment, its location kept it from much harm. The Inn's surroundings may be beautiful, but they are also functional. Between the Inn and the ocean sits a large barricade of oak trees, which helped the structure survive hurricanes like Hazel and Hugo when many other structures crumbled.

The first time I heard about the Pelican Inn, I was reading about the Gray Man of the island. Interestingly, some folks think he was never a man at all, but the spirit of a former resident of the Inn named Mrs. Mazyck. Mr. Mazyck purchased the home in 1864 during the later days of the Civil War. He held on to it until 1901. During the period he and his wife lived there, it was, for a time, used as a boarding house. Mrs. Mazyck ran a tight ship. Everyone did their part; chores were taken care of and the house was never left in a mess. The one thing that sent her blood boiling was the sight of someone loafing around. It is said she passed away in the home during those thirty-seven years, but it seems she never left after all.

She was first seen by employees of the Atlantic Coast Lumber Company, which purchased the home in 1901. The company was kind enough to allow its employees to vacation at the Inn, which for the most part I am sure they very much enjoyed. However, some of the men claimed to see an older woman glaring down at them. They knew she was not among the living because she appeared all in gray. These sightings are why some people suspected that she and the Gray Man were one and the same. Corinne Taylor, however, explained the dates do not support this claim. The first sighting of the Gray Man was in 1822, long before Mrs. Mazyck's passing. Still, it would be fair at least to give her the title of the Gray Woman. Although, instead of doing any favors for those who witness her, she is more likely to chastise you for not working.

Much like she did in life, she still runs a tight ship. It does not seem to matter that she no longer owns the home or, for that matter, is no longer alive! One former employee of the Inn was not afraid to admit that she was slacking on her job, as she retold her encounter with the Gray Woman.

While she enjoyed taking a little "break" and getting paid for it, someone noticed her inactivity. When the employee felt a distinct tap on her shoulders, she turned around to see who it was, only to find no one near her. Only slightly unnerved, she went back to leaning against the wall. She felt a second tap on her shoulder, this one stronger. Once again, she found the room empty. She then realized what had happened: the old master of the home was telling her to get back to work. Doubtlessly, telling her boss about this must have been fun for the employee.

Another employee of the home got Mrs. Mazyck's attention for another reason, however. She also got a much more powerful response. If not doing your job gets you a tap on the shoulder, then it seems using profanity while working will get Mrs. Mazyck mad as heck! A handyman of the Inn found himself alone one day, doing some routine maintenance. He ran into a few problems and, without thinking, cursed out loud. The Gray Woman, apparently, does not take lightly to profanity. The handyman looked up just in time to see a cookie sheet fly clear out of the kitchen and right at him. Not surprisingly, he left the Inn for the rest of the day and refused to return until someone else was there. To this day, he will not work in the Inn by himself and, if he is there, he makes sure to refrain from swearing. He is not too keen on invoking her wrath again.

Mrs. Mazyck once pulled off a similar trick with a kitchen knife. One has to wonder what would make her that angry. She also tends to move objects around the home, though for what purpose no one is sure. One day, a laundry hamper was found in the middle of the hallway. Only a minute before, it was in a nearby room and no one had been close to it to move it. Possibly, the Mazyck specter was attempting to take it somewhere else, but when someone walked in on her she stopped. Other items — such as coffee mugs, watches, and jewelry — will sometimes be found on completely opposite sides of the Inn. Eventually, they always turn up up where they were originally laid; after all, Mrs. Mazyck is no thief!

The last person to report actually seeing Mrs. Mazyck, or the Gray Woman, was a Mrs. Weaver in the 1960s. Weaver saw a gray apparition standing in the home, looking directly at her. Mrs. Mazyck may have never been seen again, but she still lets people know she is there.

Another spook of the area is a little sweeter than Mrs. Mazyck and haunts the outside of the house. This apparition, belonging to a little Boston terrier that died years ago saving a life, is still seen quite often to this day. His story is a heroic, but tragic, tale:

Ages ago, an older woman who lived by the Inn was out walking her two dogs, as she often did, but this time her peaceful walk was interrupted by a cry for help. She and her dogs saw a little boy struggling in the surf. There were no parents around and it appeared his only hope was the woman and her dogs. The woman was too weak to swim out and save him, but one of her dogs ran into the ocean and swam out to the boy. The child quickly grabbed hold of the dog as he turned around and headed for shore. The boy's struggling took the dog under water several times, but every time the little terrier rose back up and kept heading to the beach. Finally, they both made it and the boy was saved, but at a terrible cost. The little dog fell over on the beach and began struggling to breathe. Despite every attempt by his owner to rescue him, the dog died on the shore. The woman's other dog, now distraught, lost his will to live after his friend passed. In a few months, he would follow him into the grave.

Soon after, people started seeing a pair of Boston terriers running around the Pelican Inn. At first, most people thought they were just your typical dogs, still living and breathing…but then the dogs would become transparent and start to fade away. People will often hear a dog barking right in front of them, as if it is right at their feet, waiting for a treat. Of course, the dog is never seen, only sand and sea. Sometimes, ghostly paw prints with no owners are seen forming in the sand. It is possible the pair of friendly, ethereal dogs stay there because that is where they felt happiest in life, taking a walk on the beach. If you ever get the chance, I recommend taking a trip to the Pelican Inn — you will love it for everything that makes it so unique. A word of caution, though: Watch your language when indoors and if you hear some dogs barking when none are around do not be alarmed.

The grave of Alice Flagg.

ALICE FLAGG

MURRELLS INLET
SOUTH CAROLINA

Another well-known tale from South Carolina is that of Alice Flagg, a young woman who is said to be eternally separated from her love in part due to her family's hatred of his standing in society.

The tale of Alice Flagg starts in 1849, when her brother, Dr. Allard Flagg, moved into his new home on Murrells Inlet. His home had the prestigious name The Hermitage, and before long the doctor invited his widowed mother and sixteen-year-old sister, Alice, to live with him. Alice Flagg was a beautiful young girl with long, thick auburn hair and bright brown eyes.

Shortly after arriving, Alice took a trip into town to do some shopping, and it was during this trip that she caught the eye of a young lumberman, who came and introduced himself to her. At first, their interactions were innocent enough, but over time, the pair realized they were falling madly in love with each other.

Eventually, the young man was finally ready to officially call on Alice, which was a huge step in those days. As he entered the property, Dr. Flagg, who was in the garden, greeted and struck up a conversation with him. Dr. Flagg was a refined and well-educated man and soon discovered that his sister's young suitor was a common laborer. Dr. Flagg told the young man that he could not see his sister and demanded he leave. Once Alice found out that her family had kicked her suitor off the property, she was distraught. Soon, she started sneaking out to meet her beau in town. This continued for a while, but once again, the young man tried to visit her at home. This time he wished to take her on a nice midday carriage ride, but as Alice made her way to the door, her brother stormed out after her. He argued with Alice and the young man. Finally, though, he told them they could ride together — but only if he came along as a chaperone.

Allard Flagg rode in the carriage with Alice and forced her suitor to ride a separate horse alongside them. Throughout the ride, Dr. Flagg belittled the young man's position in society and his sister's love for him. Upon returning home, Flagg, backed up by their mother, forbade Alice from seeing him again. Warning that she would be selling her life short to be with such a commoner, they insisted she find a man of better standing.

Matters became even more complicated when the young man proposed and Alice, being in love, said yes. However, she knew her family would never agree to this, so she hid the ring by tying it to a ribbon and putting it around her neck, doubting its discovery. She got away with the deception for a time, but finally her brother noticed the ribbon around her neck and the ring on the end. Dr. Flagg took the ring from her. He became so angry with her that he shipped her off to school in Charleston. Late one night, Alice fell seriously ill. The physician concluded she had contracted malaria and instructed the school to contact her family immediately. Dr. Flagg sped to Charleston in his carriage; upon arrival, he found his sister in a delirious state. Despite the night being stormy, he packed her things and laid her in his carriage for the journey back home. The trip took over four days and, by the time they arrived, Alice's condition had worsened.

Morning came. Alice could not fight the illness and she silently went into a coma, ultimately dying a short time later. Her body was dressed in her favorite long, white dress, which a friend had sent from the school. She rested in All Saints Church Cemetery, where a plain marble slab covers her grave. The engraving on the stone consists of only one word — "Alice."

It was not long afterwards that sightings of Alice's spirit wandering the cemetery began. According to the reports, a spectral young woman, wearing a white dress, wanders around, looking for the ring her true love had given her. It is said she travels to her former home and back in her never-ending search. (Author's note: There is no information as to what became of the young suitor.)

There are also whisperings that upon visiting Alice's resting place, you should start at the bottom right corner of her gravestone and walk counterclockwise six times and then six times clockwise, before stopping at the letter "A" and placing a token of recognition upon the resting place. You then make a wish and it will be granted. Whether this ritual has merit or not, I cannot say...I have not tried it myself.

The stretch of road the ghost light is said to appear.

LAND END LIGHTS

ST. HELENA ISLAND
SOUTH CAROLINA

One certainty I have from all my years of reading about the paranormal is that every state has at least one "ghost light" story. The ghost light is that mysterious light orb that seems to drift down the road, shine from a nearby mountaintop, or appear in seemingly abandoned homes. Wherever it appears, one thing is true — it always comes with an interesting story.

The Land End Lights, seen on Land End Road, located outside Frogmore, on Saint Helena Island (Beaufort County), are South Carolina's most famous ghost lights. This stretch of road is popular with people interested in the paranormal, whether it's teenagers looking for a scare or skeptics searching for proof.

Naturally, there is an origin story for the lights; well, actually more than one. The most popular involves a Trailway bus driver during the 1940s.

One evening, in the dead of night, an exhausted bus driver traveled along the road when he permitted his eyes to rest for just a moment. This was all it took for the bus to swerve off the road...into a tree. The unfortunate driver went through the windshield and hit the ground with enough force to decapitate him.

The ghost lights were first noticed shortly after this accident. According to conjecture, the lights are the bus driver searching for his head; others claim they are his phantom bus's headlights. In addition to this, folks have reported seeing a headless apparition wandering down the road, wearing a bloodstained uniform and emitting an ethereal glow.

Another of the phenomenon's origin stories suggests that one of the oaks nearby was formerly used to hang runaway slaves, as well as an unfortunate Rebel Colonel who was lynched for looting. Supposedly, Union forces had caught him as he attempted to plunder abandoned homes in search of valuables. Now, two things normally guaranteed a quick execution during war at that time: being a spy and looting. Without trial or conviction, they hanged the colonel. When the support dropped away and he fell, his neck snapped with such force that his head popped clean off. An interesting little tidbit is that, in addition to the ghost lights, you can see his body hanging from a tree without its head.

As I have already said, countless people venture out to see the lights. Some wait hours without ever seeing anything, while others have more luck. For those who do see something, the typical experience occurs as follows:

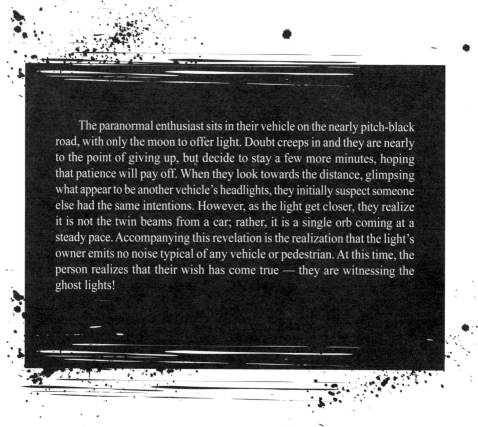

The paranormal enthusiast sits in their vehicle on the nearly pitch-black road, with only the moon to offer light. Doubt creeps in and they are nearly to the point of giving up, but decide to stay a few more minutes, hoping that patience will pay off. When they look towards the distance, glimpsing what appear to be another vehicle's headlights, they initially suspect someone else had the same intentions. However, as the light get closer, they realize it is not the twin beams from a car; rather, it is a single orb coming at a steady pace. Accompanying this revelation is the realization that the light's owner emits no noise typical of any vehicle or pedestrian. At this time, the person realizes that their wish has come true — they are witnessing the ghost lights!

How close the light draws really depends on the viewer's bravery because as soon as they crank their engine, the light vanishes. Some people have reported that the light has come as close as their car hood, even resting atop it, almost as if someone is observing the vehicle's occupants. Who or what is this ghost light, no one knows. Perhaps it is the bus driver or maybe the Colonel searching for their head. Maybe it is even a spirit unknown to the locals. Regardless of its identity, the locals love it and hope it stays around for a while.

The skeleton remains of the old church.

THE CHAPEL OF EASE

ST. HELENA ISLAND
SOUTH CAROLINA

Sitting on the small, yet beautiful island of St. Helena is the Chapel of Ease, the ruins of an old church. Constructed around 1740, it quickly became the parish church for the many planters who lived on the island. Until 1861, the majority of the town came every Sunday to worship together.

The Civil War began when South Carolina fired on Fort Sumter on April 12, 1861. Shortly after, on November 7, 1861, the Battle of Port Royal started and became an important victory for the Union. President Lincoln had called for a blockade of Confederate ports and considered Port Royal one of the most essential to be taken. A flotilla of Union ships, commanded by Samuel F. Du Pont, launched an assault on the forts defending Beaufort. However, the Union forces proved too much and, after several hours, the islands fell into their hands, where they remained throughout the war's duration.

The planters on St. Helena fled their homes when the Union came, leaving the church and nearby cemetery unprotected. It is said that some of the more rowdy soldiers, who were aching for vengeance because of the South's secession, started looting the cemetery's mausoleums. They smashed open doors and ransacked caskets for any valuables buried with the dead. In those days, it was common for a wealthy person to be buried with prized rings, watches, or cuff-links. These were things worth more than a month's pay to a poor solider.

Among the dead interred in the cemetery were the Fripps, the chapel's oftentimes caretakers. Edgar Fripp and his wife, Eliza, had passed away shortly after their mausoleum was completed; their bodies laid near the church they had spent every Sunday in attendance. When the soldiers ransacked the grounds, their tomb was smashed open and torn apart. Their bodies were robbed of everything, including their dignity. The damage done to the graveyard was left untended, as people deemed its destruction trivial in comparison to the carnage going on in the war around them.

After the war, the people examined the damage. The Chapel was fine (although it would be destroyed in 1868 by a forest fire), largely due to the fact it had been used every Sunday by troops stationed there, much like the planters had before them. When the people began their repairs of the mausoleums, they seemed to run into a problem with Edgar and Eliza's. The workers bricked up the entrance to their mausoleum. As the night dragged on, they decided they would wait to retrieve all their tools until morning, when they had more light.

When they returned, the workers found that half the bricks had been removed from the entrance and stacked very neatly next to it, almost as if it had been left half completed the day before. At first they were not spooked, but angry, assuming some vandal had shown up after they left and undid their work for a laugh. They contacted the caretaker, who assured them that no one had been on the grounds after they left, and reassured the workers that it would have been impossible for someone to remove those bricks without him hearing it. On top of that, all their tools had been left untouched, a sign that vandals had not been there, as this would have been something to steal and sell off for profit.

Realizing they would never figure out how or why, the workers put the other half of the bricks back over the entrance. Once again, they finished their job, leaving it fully sealed up for the second time. This time they took the tools with them, in case whomever took the bricks down showed back up and decided to use them.

The next day, the, caretaker found the bricks removed and placed in a neat pile once again. He sent word to the workers for them to return. Upon their arrival, they accused the caretaker of sleeping through his duties and allowing the vandalism to occur...twice! The story goes that the workers tried several more times to replace the bricks. Each time they would return to find them removed and the bricks neatly stacked by the entrance. They even tried to catch the culprits by having someone watch the mausoleum during the night. The entrance remained sealed the whole time he was there, but between the time he left and when the caretaker inspected later, they were removed. They finally gave up, maybe accepting that something supernatural was taking place. The mausoleum remains half-covered up to this day.

Who exactly is haunting that mausoleum? Is it the Fripps or, possibly, the Union soldiers reliving their ransacking of the tomb? Whoever it is, they made it clear they want it left open.

The cemetery and chapel have other specters walking the grounds. The specters are seen both in the dark night and in the brightness of day. Visitors see people, in Victorian clothing, out for a stroll on the grounds. They make no noise and appear as solid as any living person appears, although one witness stated it did not look like the man she saw was walking, but rather *gliding* across the grounds. They are seen normally walking (or gliding) towards the old church's entrance, as if they are simply heading to Sunday service.

As is common with such sightings, the ghostly churchgoers vanish as soon as they get near the structure. Still, there are times when people drawing near the chapel's empty shell hear the sound of soft prayers and whispering coming from inside, as if church was in session. They are never seen, and if you actually enter, it will go silent.

There are a number of entities walking the grounds, but the one that stands out the most is that of what appears to be a young mother and child. Unlike most of the spooks seen wearing dark-colored clothing, she is seen in a white dress and carrying her small child. She never seems to be trying to reach the chapel; rather, she darts through the graveyard in some kind of daze, seemingly unaware of her somber surroundings. Who she is and what she is doing there is anyone's guess, as she always makes sure to vanish before anyone can get too near. Maybe she was a grief-stricken mother who lost her child and, in death, attempts to reunite with him...but that is just a guess.

If you ever find yourself near the Chapel of Ease, make sure to keep an eye and ear open for the local spooks. However, this is not the only haunted church ruins in the area — nearby Beaufort has its own equally mysterious former house of God.

The ghostly and trouble-making Jester.

OLD SHELDON CHURCH

BEAUFORT
SOUTH CAROLINA

Located on Old Sheldon Church Road, the church's gutted ruins sit in the midst of Spanish moss-covered trees and scattered graves. You cannot ask for a better setting for a haunting, as it looks like a scene from a classic ghost story. Sometime around 1745, the original building was constructed and originally named Prince William Parish, a common signal of loyalty to the monarch at that time. However, when loyalty disappeared in the American Revolution, the British burned the church down in 1779. In some ways, this was fitting; when the war ended, the Americans rebuilt the church — it rose from the ashes like a phoenix, and received its current name, free of its former British ties. Once again, the church prospered, and for many decades, served as the site for the townspeople's happy occasions.

As seems to be the general case, it all changed in the final days of the Civil War, during Sherman's razing of the South. Local legend originally held that, just as the British had done decades before, Sherman had the church burned to the ground. This was very easy to believe since he burned much of the town, not to mention a large portion of the South. Arson and Sherman went together like peanut butter and jelly — churches were not exempt from his torches.

However, this claim was actually disproved in the last few decades. A letter was uncovered, dating back to February 3, 1866, telling how the church fared in 1865. According to the author, the church was not burned down at all. Only the church's interior was destroyed by the rampaging soldiers. They could have repaired the church, but it seemed that the residents decided to use the wood and supplies from the structure to rebuild their own homes. After all, what good is having a church to go to on Sunday if you have nowhere to go the other six days of the week?

For the longest time, the ruins sat unkempt, becoming overgrown, until it resembled something from a horror movie. Eventually, the grounds were cleaned up. They are now a popular site for people to visit on a bright spring day. In fact, the ruins are still used for some of the church's original purpose: weddings still take place on occasion, presumably for those who cannot decide if they want a church or outdoor wedding.

Even so, it is not all happy events at the old church. There are whisperings that at least one specter inhabits the church. No one knows when she was first seen, but the ghost — a woman dressed in a worn, dirty brown dress — is often seen crying by an old grave. She appears conflicted by deep depression, but when anyone approaches to offer her comfort, she quickly disappears from sight. Some have claimed to see her slowly walking with her head tilted towards the ground. An unearthly crying accompanies her whenever anyone sees her.

Another common belief is that the woman is responsible for other odd occurrences, such as bizarre floating lights seen on the grounds at night and unusual light phenomena in photos taken there, including orbs, light beams, and even gray mist. People also report sometimes hearing footsteps within the church, described as heavy and booted. There is debate as to whether these belong to the woman or some other entity.

Many people claim she is a war widow who is so distraught over her husband's falling in battle she still visits his grave in death. She is not seen too often now, although people continue to feel her presence…a deep, sorrowful feeling overcomes people in certain locations, before simply vanishing as they continue onward. Additionally, people continue to hear weeping, though she may remain hidden from view.

Those who have ventured to the location at night report even more odd scenes. Black shadowy figures — almost like living shadows — are said to dart past the graves and trees. Those who attempt to use cameras often will have their batteries die, going from fully charged to empty in a matter of moments. Despite the camera problems, none of the activity seems to pose any harm…they simply may scare you and send you running if you go sightseeing at night.

The ghostly and trouble-making Jester.

GAUCHE THE HUGUENOT GHOST

BEAUFORT
SOUTH CAROLINA

Here is a story a little more on the bizarre side. It's a story of a ghost of a small man who, depending on which version you believe, died in a horrific way. I must admit, this is one of the stories I enjoyed reading about the most. It has a little bit of history, mystery, and, of course, a ghost. The first thing you need to know about is the time that the ghost is said to be from — the time of the Huguenots.

The Huguenots were members of the Protestant Reformed Church of France who were inspired by John Calvin's writings in the 1530s. By the end of the seventeenth century and into the eighteenth century, roughly 500,000 Huguenots had fled France because of a series of religious persecutions, relocating to Protestant nations such as England, Scotland, Denmark, and the English's North American colonies (just to name a few).

That brings us to Jean Ribault (1520–October 12, 1565), a French naval officer and Huguenot born in Dieppe, on the English Channel, in the Province of Normandy. He entered the French navy under the command of the great Huguenot admiral Gaspard de Coligny. In 1562, he led an expedition to the New World in order to found a colony. He left France on February 18th with a fleet of 150 men. He crossed the Atlantic Ocean and, beginning his search in Florida, started working his way up the coastline. Eventually, they came to the Port Royal Sound in present-day South Carolina, where Ribault decided to establish a settlement on modern-day Parris Island, an island located on the coast. He founded Charlesport, which was named after the King of France, Charles IX. Ribault left twenty-seven colonists behind and headed back towards France for more supplies.

Among the colonists there was supposedly a midget named Gauche. A jester by trade, Gauche was brought along to entertain the men on the long trip. In the days before television or even radio, jesters were in high demand. Many stories exist about this small entertainer and, although varied, they all seem to have an unhappy end for him. Shortly after their comrade's departure, the colonists became so overwhelmed by the New World's harshness that they became far more savage. One account states that the jester was involved in a fight with two others; though the reasons behind it are lost, it is suggested that one of the men mortally stabbed him. Another, more disturbing story involving his demise is that once conditions got so bad at the failing colony, the men decided to abandon it. They made a crude ship and set sail for France. However, once their food ran out, the men killed and ate Gauche!

Granted, no tangible historic evidence exists to support that Gauche even existed, but that is not altogether surprising, as Ribault wrote the only account of his voyage while held prisoner in the Tower of London. He never mentioned a jester, though this could be due to purposeful omission or lapse of memory, just as easily as it could be due to the midget's nonexistence.

Long after Ribault's failed colony, around the 1850s, a certain Dr. Joseph Johnson built a house known as The Castle at 411 Craven Street in Beaufort. Before the house was even completed, Union forces seized it and utilized it as a military hospital and morgue. This was not the intended beginning for the home, but when the war ended, it was returned to Johnson's family.

Although many former military hospitals seem to have their fair share of ghosts, the ghost that haunts The Castle supposedly has nothing to do with the Civil War. The earliest accounts of a ghost came from Dr. Johnson and his staff. His gardener would feel uneasy as he tended the yard, as if someone was watching him. Dr. Johnson actually claimed to see the midget jester, Gauche, walking in his yard, dressed in a pointed hat with bells on his shoes. His daughter, Mrs. Lily Danner, got more than a peek at the ghostly jester. As a child, she supposedly had tea parties with him all the time and described him as an older man, dressed as her father had stated. She also claimed he would tap out messages in Morse code, often filled with profanity and criticisms of those living in the house.

Often, he moved various sized furniture around the home. He did this with Dee Hryharrow, a resident in the 1940s. Despite never fully believing in ghosts, she was at a loss as to how to explain the oddities occurring. One day, while she was alone, after leaving the room for only a few moments, she returned to find her child's crib wedged in front of the door, which made it nearly impossible for her to open it. Based on the manner done, there was no way for someone to bar the door and then depart the room; however, when she finally worked her way into the room, it was empty. When she was pregnant with her second child, Dee endured another experience that was just as equally difficult to explain.

She had been lying in bed most of the day as she waited for her son's arrival, as she had received word of his impending visit. When she heard the front door open, followed by footsteps coming up the stairs and down the hall, as if someone was drawing towards her, she assumed it was her son. She called out to him, but when she did not receive a response, she investigated. To her surprise, the hallway was empty…as if whoever the footsteps belonged to had vanished when he/she reached her door.

The phantom has made his presence known to many others as well, often seen as a smoky figure or leaving red handprints on windows. One of the most unusual events attributed to Gauche took place in 1969; locals know it as "The Roast Ghost." A resident of a nearby home had just cooked a roast when she had to leave to take her maid home. Upon her return, the woman realized the roast had disappeared. She could find no evidence of forced entry, yet the roast was inexplicably gone. Not too much later, another resident had her roast stolen in the same manner. Though it is possible that there is a logical explanation for the food's disappearance, such as some hungry vagabond making his way into the kitchen, following his nose, there are folks who prefer the ghostly jester explanation.

Nonetheless, the story of this non-corporal jester has survived since the earliest days of The Castle and is not likely to be going anywhere anytime soon!

THE BATTERY

CHARLESTON
SOUTH CAROLINA

No city in South Carolina boasts more specters per mile than the grand port city of Charleston. Countless bars, homes, and restaurants are home to earthbound souls from the city's past. Scores of books have been written on the ghosts of this city alone and it's easy to see why. After all, Charleston is such a beautiful place, why would anyone, dead or living, want to leave?

Most Charleston residents will state that White Point Gardens is home to the city's most terrifying and interesting entities. The moss-laden White Point Gardens (also known as Battery Park or just "The Battery") is filled with mighty oak statues. It is in this beautiful park where, for four days in 1718, Stede Bonnet and twenty-eight members of his crew were hanged for their crimes. Their corpses were left swaying in the wind for any curious eye to see.

America has something of a love affair with pirates. Countless movies have heralded them as antiheroes or antagonized them as ruthless villains. The many books about them prove they are one of our favorite types of villains. Something about sailing the high seas and robbing ships speaks to our inner rebel. Along with these stories of the bloodthirsty pirates comes the sub-category of ghost pirate stories, which even in the days of piracy were common. Blackbeard alone is said to haunt several locations in North and South Carolina. Stories say he had a run-in with the devil the day he died. Of course, Blackbeard is not the only pirate whose ghost has garnered popularity. There is also Stede Bonnet.

Stede Bonnet (c. 1688–December 10, 1718) started his life as a wealthy landowner before turning to his life of piracy. Bonnet was born on the island of Barbados to a rich English family and became master of their estate upon his father's death in 1694. In 1709, he married Mary Allamby, and later served time with the militia. Unfortunately, his marriage was not a happy one. Due to his marital problems, and despite his lack of sailing experience, Bonnet decided to turn to piracy in the summer of 1717. He bought a sailing vessel, named it *Revenge*, and traveled with his paid crew along the Eastern Seaboard of what is now the United States. During their journeys, they captured other vessels and robbed them for all they could.

Soon after, Bonnet set sail for Nassau in the Bahamas; however, he encountered a Spanish warship. The ensuing battle seriously wounded him. Regardless of this delay, the *Revenge* arrived in Nassau, where Bonnet would meet the infamous Edward Teach, better known as Blackbeard. Due to his injury, Bonnet felt he could not command his vessel and temporarily gave command to Teach. Sometime after this, when Bonnet was back commanding his ship again, he attempted but failed to capture the ship *Protestant Caesar*. In disgust, his crew abandoned him and joined Black Beard permanently aboard the *Queen Anne's Revenge*. Now lacking a crew, Stede also went aboard Blackbeard's ship as a guest.

While on board the *Queen Anne*, Bonnet received a pardon by North Carolina governor Charles Eden. Moreover, he received permission to work as a privateer against the Spanish merchant ships for the crown. This boon of fortune came about in June 1718, when the mighty *Queen Anne's Revenge* ran aground off the coast of North Carolina and put the feared pirate in a very vulnerable state.

Blackbeard ordered Bonnet and a few other men to speak with the local authorities in Bath. They intended to get pardons for themselves by agreeing to give up their pirating ways. Having been raised in the ways of a gentleman, Bonnet successfully completed his negotiations and, full of pride, made his way back to the stranded ship. However, he soon found the *Queen Anne* had long gone. Blackbeard had pulled a typical pirate move — made off with most of his crew and all the loot they had collected. In this line of work, unlucky stragglers were commonly left behind; Bonnet and a handful of his loyal crew found themselves in such an unfortunate situation.

Bonnet and his few remaining men set sail once again in the *Revenge*. He had no treasure to pay his men or even food to feed them, so that left only one choice: Return to his pirating ways. He, of course, wished to preserve his pardon, so he changed the name of the *Revenge* to the *Royal James* and referred to himself as Captain Thomas to those he robbed. At this point, he still knew nothing about sailing or commanding, leaving the role of commander to quartermaster Robert Tucker. From July to September 1718, Bonnet saw the high point of his piratical career — in that time he had captured several vessels off the Atlantic Seaboard.

In August 1718, Bonnet anchored the *Royal James* for repair work on an estuary of the Cape Fear River. In late September, Colonel William Rhett, by authority of South Carolina governor Robert Johnson, led a naval expedition against pirates on the river. He soon found the *Royal James* still under repair and attacked the vulnerable ship without hesitation. Rhett and Bonnet's men fought each other for hours, but the outnumbered pirates ultimately surrendered when their supplies began to run low. Rhett arrested the pirates and brought them to Charleston in early October. Bonnet escaped on October 24th, but was recaptured on Sullivan's Island shortly afterward. On November 10th, Bonnet went to trial, during which authorities charged him with two acts of piracy. Judge Nicholas Trott sentenced Bonnet to death. The condemned pirate wrote to Governor Johnson to ask for clemency, but Johnson endorsed the judge's decision. In the end, Bonnet, along with his men, was hanged in Charleston on December 10, 1718. Finally, Bonnet's ability to weasel his way out trouble failed him.

Since that day, people near the sturdy oaks of White Point at night may see the bodies of Bonnet's crew still hanging…with the men's dead eyes set on them! Some

Stede Bonnet meets his fate at the gallows.

folks even claim to hear the disembodied laughter of those ghostly scoundrels. Who knows? Perhaps the specters' dark mirth serves to mock those who thought a mere hanging would put an end to their evil. Bonnet and his men are also said to be responsible for the shadowy figures seen in the area. They dart past trees in a blur and will sometimes run by people, giving them a scare of a lifetime! When Bonnet and his men are present, abnormal levels of fear and anxiety apparently overcome people. The sudden terror comes out of nowhere and disappears just as quickly. I myself have been to the Battery several times and cannot claim to have had the fortune (or misfortune, depending on how you see it) of experiencing these phenomena. Every time I am in Charleston — now and in the future — I plan to stop by and see if I can finally change that!

Customers arrive at the popular eatery Poogan's Porch. Might they catch a glimpse of a ghostly entity as they enjoy their "spirits"?

POOGAN'S PORCH

CHARLESTON
SOUTH CAROLINA

Poogan's Porch is the culinary Mecca of Charleston. It is not only a delight for the taste buds of locals and tourists, but for well-known celebrities and politicians as well. Even an initial glance at Poogan's will reveal that it began as a home and not a business. It was built as a spacious Victorian home in 1888. Although the identity of its builder is speculative, I can tell you with certainty that they only stayed there for around twelve years.

Around 1900, two of the home's most famous residents moved in: Zoe St. Aman and her sister, Elizabeth. Zoe, born in Charleston in 1879, worked as a schoolteacher, a profession one can easily guess by her picture. Her former pupils remembered her as a stern educator, unforgiving towards their mistakes. Neither Zoe nor her sister ever married, but they enjoyed each other's company as lifelong friends. In 1945, though, their lives would drastically change.

At this time, as the Second World War was drawing to a violent close, Elizabeth passed away, leaving Zoe by herself. Grief wracked Zoe so violently that she shut herself off from everyone else. Already a solitary individual even before her sister's passing, Zoe started to lose her mind. Neighbors reported seeing her seated figure staring out from the upstairs window, perhaps waiting for someone's cherished return home.

Occasionally, Zoe would call out her sister's name, hoping Elizabeth would come back and ease away her sorrow. As Zoe's mental and physical state worsened, her neighbors realized she could no longer take care of herself. The neighbors decided to do what was best for Zoe, and took her to St. Francis Hospital to live out the remainder of her days, which, sadly, wasn't that long. She died shortly after her admittance to St. Francis in 1954. In the end, Zoe only outlived her sister by nine years. Zoe's body now rests in St. Lawrence Cemetery, at 60 Huguenin Avenue, in Charleston.

In 1976, the owners of the St. Aman sisters' former home sold it to Bobbie Ball. Bobbie, however, did not wish to reside there. He had a vision to transform the home into a restaurant. While the house was undergoing its conversion, a little dog, Poogan, enjoyed his status as a friendly pooch in the neighborhood. He walked from home to home, looking for some table scraps, which the people lovingly offered to him. Once it was established, Bobbie's new restaurant would be no exception.

In fact, Bobbie must have spoiled Poogan with food, as the dog made his home right on the front porch, essentially becoming the greeter for approaching customers. The staff and customers loved him so much they decided to name the restaurant after him. In 1979, Poogan died of natural causes. He had become such a fixture of the place that his loved ones laid him to rest on the property.

Since it opened its door to the public over three decades ago, Poogan's has not only established its reputation for food, but also for its ghostly residents who appear from time to time. Poogan, the beloved mascot of the restaurant, is often seen sitting on the porch as he did while alive. Upon their approach to the entrance, customers can see the cute little dog relaxing at the end of the porch...but he vanishes in an instant. Even after his death, Poogan is always welcome on the porch of the restaurant. However, the most active spook at Poogan's is Zoe, who likes to remind people that this is still *her* house.

Across the street is a hotel called The Mill House, where guests sometimes notice an aged, black-garbed woman staring out of Poogan's window. Once, a hotel guest saw this woman and assumed she was a customer of the restaurant who had somehow been locked in. The longer the guest stared, the more he noticed how sadness clung to the woman's features. His heart ached for her. The guest called the Charleston police and reported the poor woman to them, but when the authorities arrived they found no sign of the woman in black.

Another encounter involved a handyman who arrived at Poogan's hours before the start of business to get some repairs done. Completely alone at the time, he fixed himself a cup of coffee and began his duties. A sudden noise from the kitchen tore away his attention. The ensuing racket implied that every pot, pan, plate, and utensil was falling on the floor at once. The handyman's first thought was that the roof had collapsed. He quickly ran towards the kitchen to survey the damage, but upon bursting through the doors, he found everything in perfect order. He could find neither fork nor spoon on the spotless floor, so what had been the cause for the previous loud commotion? A little shaken — to say the least — he headed back towards the dining room. The confused handyman returned to his tools, picked up his coffee, and started to take a sip while he gathered his nerves. Startlingly, he found every drop of coffee gone and the sheen of red lipstick on the rim of the cup!

In the encounter with the handyman, Zoe clearly decided to stay hidden, but she has been seen a number of times by others. She appears at different places. People have spotted her walking up the stairs to the second floor, standing on the stairs between floors, and in the upstairs doorway facing Queen Street. One hostess at Poogan's managed to get even closer to Zoe, much to the living woman's dismay. It had been a busy night for the restaurant, but it had finally died down. The staff was getting ready to close for the evening. During her work, the young hostess saw an older woman in a black dress walk by her station. Nearing closing time or not, Poogan's staff had to take care of their customers, so, naturally, the hostess tried to get the woman's attention in order to seat her. However, the woman merely headed towards the dining room by herself, unfazed by the hostess's hospitality. Of course, the hostess followed her in. She found the black-clad woman sitting in the otherwise vacant dining room. The hostess asked her if she would care for something to drink as she looked at the menu. The mysterious customer looked directly at the hostess, smiled faintly, and then faded away into thin air. No doubt, the young woman was beyond shocked! If she had not been ready to end her shift before her ghostly encounter, she certainly was anxious to flee home afterwards.

Other employees have also run into Zoe. Quite a number of these meetings involved chefs who had worked in the restaurant by their lonesome. To this day, customers and dining room staff will sometimes feel her cold, whispering touch as she walks by them or shortly places her hand on their backs.

With all of these incidents, it should come as no surprise that Bobbie Ball also had an experience with Zoe. He recounted a story from not too long ago. In his own words:

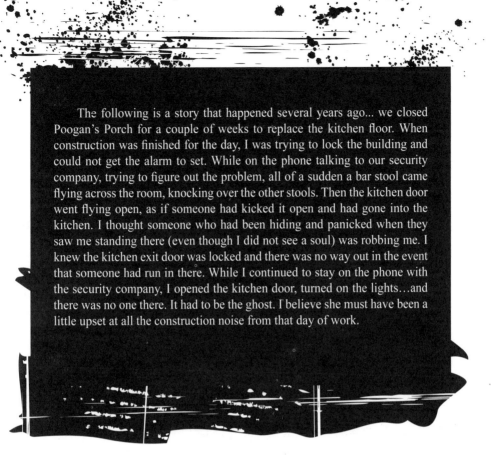

The following is a story that happened several years ago... we closed Poogan's Porch for a couple of weeks to replace the kitchen floor. When construction was finished for the day, I was trying to lock the building and could not get the alarm to set. While on the phone talking to our security company, trying to figure out the problem, all of a sudden a bar stool came flying across the room, knocking over the other stools. Then the kitchen door went flying open, as if someone had kicked it open and had gone into the kitchen. I thought someone who had been hiding and panicked when they saw me standing there (even though I did not see a soul) was robbing me. I knew the kitchen exit door was locked and there was no way out in the event that someone had run in there. While I continued to stay on the phone with the security company, I opened the kitchen door, turned on the lights…and there was no one there. It had to be the ghost. I believe she must have been a little upset at all the construction noise from that day of work.

It is not uncommon for some haunts to get bent out of shape when any remodeling is being done on their homes. Obviously, Zoe, who occupies both past and present, still sees Poogan's as her home. After all, she can never leave the place. Could anyone blame her for her actions, when she is forced to see her own home change without her permission? There can be little doubt that Zoe haunts her former home, and it would seem she is aware of her astral state and of the living people around her. For all we living know, Zoe may take care of Poogan as he still sits on the porch. At least she will never be lonely again, and Poogan will never be without the attention his canine kind so often need. They both have all of eternity to share each other's company.

The Old City Jail.

OLD CITY JAIL

CHARLESTON
SOUTH CAROLINA

We have all, at least once in our lives, seen a place that seems to scream "haunted." It may be an old abandoned home, an overgrown cemetery, or, in one particular case, a huge stone jail. The Old City Jail of Charleston has a long and bloody history, and its terrifying interior and exterior certainly match its past. I first visited the jail two years ago during a ghost tour. I have been on numerous haunted city tours and I can definitely say the jail proved to be one of my favorites. It left a strong impression on me for three reasons: one, its appearance is fittingly creepy; two, the tour guides were great; and three, and most important of all, its history is fascinating!

Even before the current structure was built upon it, the land has had a troubled past. The first known structure placed there was a workhouse for slaves; it also doubled as a hospital for paupers. Considering the medicine used in those days, the poor would have been better off staying away. Frightening reports emerge from history, and they speak of punishments carried out on both slaves and criminals. Those who were interned here had been whipped and branded, drawn, and quartered.

Construction began on the current building in 1790, and the jail was finally opened in 1802. At the time of its completion, it was meant to hold roughly 130 people. However, it seldom had less than three hundred prisoners. Some of Charleston's worst undesirables served time here. Moreover, many were brought to the gallows in the jail's courtyard and executed. During the Civil War, military prisoners were also held here. POWs included surviving members of the 54th Massachusetts, caught after their July 18, 1863, attack on Fort Wagner. The foreboding stone structure would continue to serve as a jail until its closing in 1939.

Even at its closing, the jail still lacked plumbing or electricity. It is estimated that nearly 10,000 people died during its 137-year span. The Old City Jail would sit vacant for sixty-one years until, in 2000, the American College of the Building Arts acquired it. Upon acquisition, the college initiated an emergency stabilization program to meet the immediate needs of this historic property. To this day, the college is working on restoring the jail, which is a hub of activity during the day, as the people work on repairs, and at night, when folks come for the ghost tours.

When I took the tour, the guide showed us the dismal cells that once held mobs of prisoners in claustrophobic quarters. I imagined that, for those captured souls, every moment in the jail was a nightmare. One of the guides shared an interesting tidbit of information. Apparently, the staircase has thirteen steps, all of which are badly worn, except for the first. Our guide explained how the prisoners had been a superstitious group: to avoid stepping on all thirteen steps, the jail's doomed captives would skip the first one. According to the tour guide, the students working in the day would see and hear the strangest things. Frightened, most of them refused to stay in the basement area alone.

Later in the tour, we reached the most important room of the jail — the area where Lavinia Fisher, America's first female serial killer, was kept. Not surprisingly, it is said she also haunts her old room, which was nearly pitch-black during the tour. Fortunately, I had brought a camcorder fitted with an infrared lens, so I was able to see the room as the tour continued. At last, I saw what might have been something paranormal: a white orb moving around the room. When the guide first mentioned Lavinia's name, the orb moved close to him and hovered there for a moment. Human reason could write the orb off as a bug. However, our tour was on a cold October night, so the bug theory is not without its flaws. While I studied the now-moving orb, our guide retold the story of Lavinia, the cold-blooded beauty who had occupied the room 190 years before we did.

Few solid statements can be made of Lavinia Fisher. What is certain is her birth year — 1793 — but the location of her birth, her maiden name, or any information about her childhood is lost to the ages. Nothing of her life is known until she married a man named John Fisher. The couple settled near Charleston, where they made their living operating a hotel called the Six Mile Wayfarer House. Its name came from its location — six miles outside of Charleston.

In that day, highwaymen infested any roads leading to such a major port city like Charleston. Regardless, even the countless highwaymen could not account for the abnormal number of missing visitors. People in Charleston would be expecting friends or family to be riding in any day, only to never see them show up. As more reports of failed visitors came in and the authorities claimed these people missing, it was determined that they were last seen at the Six Mile Wayfarer House. Though the local authorities began an investigation, there was no evidence that the Fishers were involved. This, coupled with their popularity in the town, led to the investigation being dropped.

Lavinia was a very beautiful and charming woman, which not only boosted her favor in the community, but the business of the Six Mile Wayfarer House, as well. Soon, the public would discover that she used those talents to aid her dark deeds. Because Lavinia's beauty put travelers at ease, they unwittingly told her everything she needed to know. Eventually, the locals tired of the authorities' lackluster action and gathered a group of vigilantes. The group went to the Fishers' in February 1819 to stop the activities occurring there. Although it is not known what happened when they encountered the Fishers, the mob eventually departed without incident, leaving one man named David Ross to stand watch in the area. Serial killers are often dangerously charismatic and persuasive. It is possible, then, that Lavinia worked her charm on the angry mob of locals.

Early the next morning, two men attacked David Ross and dragged him before a group of people. In that group was none other than Lavinia Fisher. Ross looked to her for help. Instead, Fisher choked him and smashed his head through a window. Realizing he may soon be dead, Ross made a run for it — he was successful in his escape and was able to alert authorities.

Shortly after this incident, a man named John Peeples was traveling from Georgia to Charleston. Tired from his long trip, he stopped at the Six Mile House to see if they had a room. He was warmly greeted by the beautiful Lavinia when he knocked on the door. The attractive killer informed him they had no vacancies, but invited him in for tea and a meal. Peeples found her company so pleasant that he ignored the odd glances of Lavinia's husband. Sure enough, Peeples answered Lavinia's every question without fail. When she excused herself from the table for a moment, she returned with tea and good news. A room had suddenly become available if John still wanted it. He accepted, and Lavinia poured him a cup of tea.

Luckily, John did not like tea, but he did not want to seem impolite. Instead of refusing it or leaving it untouched, he poured it out when she was not looking. Afterward, she showed him to his room. Only now did Peeples begin to wonder why she had asked him so many questions. Moreover, why had her husband been staring at him all evening? Suddenly, a deep sense of foreboding struck Peebles and he suspected he might soon become a victim of robbery. Feeling safer in the chair by the door than in the bed, he dozed until a loud noise awoke him a few hours later. Looking around, he realized that the bed he should have been sleeping in had disappeared, swallowed by a deep hole beneath the floor. He had not misplaced his worries, after all. Alarmed, Peeples quickly jumped out the window, straddled his horse, and fled to authorities in Charleston. After the appearance of two reports directly incriminating the Fishers, the police finally arrested John and Lavinia Fisher. Two men who had been assisting the Fishers were also arrested.

Later, authorities thoroughly searched the Six Mile Wayfarer House and dug up the grounds. The dig revealed hidden, underground passages. The sheriff reportedly found items that could be traced to dozens of travelers in the attic, which could only be accessed by a secret passageway. He also found tea laced with a herb that induced sleep for hours, a mechanism that could be triggered to open the floorboards beneath the bed, and, in the basement, hundreds of human remains.

Despite the mountain of evidence, the Fishers pled not guilty. Still, the pair was ordered to stay in jail until their trial. In the meantime, their co-conspirators were released on bail. At the Fishers' trial in May, the jury saw through their flimsy plea of innocence. Ultimately, the Fishers were found guilty of multiple counts of highway robbery and they were sentenced to hang. However, they were given time to appeal the conviction.

During the wait, they occupied themselves by planning their escape. Housed together in a loosely guarded jail, they started making a rope from jail linens. On September 13th, they executed their plan and used the rope to drop down to the ground. John made it out, but the rope broke, leaving Lavinia trapped in the cell. Proving that even the worst of us can love someone, John would not leave without his wife. As a result, he was recaptured and returned to the jail, where they were now kept under much tighter security. In February 1820, the Constitutional Court rejected the Fishers' appeal and their execution was scheduled for later that month.

A local minister named Reverend Richard Furman was sent in to counsel the pair, if they were open to it. After all, salvation only comes to the willing. John freely talked to Furman and is said to have pleaded with the Reverend to save his soul, if not his life. However, Lavinia was so angry and bitter, she would have nothing to do with him or his God. On the morning of February 18, 1820, the Fishers were taken from the Old City Jail to be hanged on the gallows behind the building. John Fisher went quietly, praying with the minister, whom he had asked to read a letter. Before a crowd of some 2,000 people, the letter insisted he was innocent and asked for mercy on those who had done him wrong in the judicial process. He then began to plead his case before the gathered crowd, but before he was hanged, he asked for the crowd's forgiveness, possibly contradicting his earlier statement.

Because it was illegal to execute a married woman, John was hanged first, thereby making Lavinia a widow. The now-unmarried woman did not go as quietly as her husband did. She had requested to wear her wedding dress and even refused to walk to the gallows. Instead, she would be picked up and carried as she ranted and raved. Before the crowd, she continued to scream pointedly at the Charleston socialites, whom she blamed for encouraging her conviction. Before her executioners could tighten the noose around her neck, she yelled into the crowd, "If you have a message you want to send to hell, give it to me—I'll carry it," and before they could finish the job, she jumped off the scaffold herself. Not quite reaching the ground, she dangled down into the crowd. Later, onlookers would say they had never seen such a wicked stare or chilling sneer as that which was on 27-year-old Lavinia's face. The Fishers were buried in Potters Field Cemetery, very close to where they had been executed.

Lavinia's ghost has been seen for well over a hundred years, most often in the wedding dress she died in. Prisoners would report seeing a woman in a white dress roaming the halls or even appearing in the cells with them. Under normal circumstances, a bunch of locked-up men would love to have a woman in their cells. Yet, under these supernatural circumstances, they found her terrifying. Lavinia's cold, negative energy could be felt by all around her. Even after the jail closed, those walking by would sometimes see a woman staring back at them from the dark windows of the building. At other times, her figure walks away from the jail. Her person looks so tangible that witnesses can only assume a wedding is being held there that day.

I had a chance to talk with Eric Lavender, one of the jail's tour guides, who shared some interesting stories about ghostly encounters experienced by tourists. The first story took place about five years ago. A group was near an area formerly occupied by an octagonal tower, which was added in 1855. This tower was badly damaged on September 1, 1886, by a 7.3 earthquake and had to be removed. The group began hearing what sounded like a great mass of people running around on the floor above them. In such a complex building, the location of everyone must be known so that if anyone is hurt they can be found easily. Therefore, the tour guides were certain no one occupied the upper floors at the time, but then they noticed dust falling from the ceiling and by the nearby window, as if the building was shaking. It is possible that when the earthquake hit, it caused such a panic that some poor souls had been doomed to relive that day repeatedly.

The stomping spirits are not normally heard often. However, a frequently reoccurring entity appears as a black, shadowy figure. It runs from one end of the jail to the other. One guide recalled a recent incident with this elusive spook. The guide was giving his tour near an open door, when he saw a shadow dart by the open door. He first thought his eyes were playing tricks on him, so he simply continued his story…but every time he looked by the door the black shadow would be there one instant and then dart back around the corner again. This game of peek-a-boo went on the entire time he was in that room. Such an event did not stand out as extraordinary, though; shadow figures are frequently seen by guides, tourists, and students in the building. When seen at certain angles, the shadow figures seem to be peering into rooms, as if keeping an eye on the people within.

The dark ghosts' abilities go well beyond just peeking around corners and making a little noise. One of the specters seems to be stronger than at least two grown men. Once, Eric and another guide were in the building, giving a tour. In the middle of the tour, they reached the door that led to Lavinia's old cell. Opening the door is normally a simple task, but try as he might to open it, Eric could not even get it to budge. Seeing Eric struggle, his fellow guide gave him a hand. Even then, with the strength of two men combined, the door did not open. The two guides finally gave up and simply skipped Lavinia's room. They assumed something had been wedged in the door, and would only be removed through a lot of effort. However, when the next tour came through about thirty minutes later, the door opened without a problem. Perhaps the ghost behind that portal was simply not in the mood for company earlier.

A young man who had been on a tour a few years ago recounted an odd happening while waiting for the tour to start. He had reached the Old City Jail early and was looking around outside. As he walked towards the back of the building, he heard what sounded like wood slamming together, followed by clapping and loud whispers. The young man could not make out what was being said. The voices quickly stopped as he neared the back. He later discovered that the area once contained the gallows. At this point, he was convinced that he had heard the ambiance of a long-past hanging.

Since its reopening, the jail has been visited by many paranormal investigation groups. Although the groups' evidence varies, the investigators never seem to come away empty-handed, so the next time you find yourself in Charleston, make sure to take a ghost tour of the Old City Jail. You will not be disappointed.

The Unitarian Church.

THE HAUNTED
UNITARIAN CHURCH

CHARLESTON
SOUTH CAROLINA

Almost all visitors to Charleston have seen the Unitarian church on Archdale Street. It is a marvelous old building with magnetic appeal. The church also has a cemetery, which has more or less been turned into a beautiful garden. I am a fan of historic cemeteries; they hold the mortal remains of people who lived during some of the most important times in history. Out of all the cemeteries I have visited, the Unitarian church's is my favorite. Both beauty and sadness dwell there in quiet peace. On my first visit there, I had no idea it was supposed to be haunted — I just wanted to admire its beauty. Although I never saw anything, I felt eyes watching me. I was pretty picture happy with my camera, so perhaps someone was giving me the stink eye. At least, that is what I told myself. On my second visit, I learned about both the history and the ghosts of the old church.

It was 1772, just four years before the signing of the Declaration of Independence, that the Society of Dissenters, known today as the Circular Congregational Church, was growing. The rate of growth required the Society to gather more space for its followers. Though they had a church on Meeting Street, the building's size was not sufficient. Therefore, the Society had no choice but to expand by adding a second building on Archdale Street. Construction started that year, and by the time the Revolution was starting, the job was nearly done. Unfortunately, the war brought the building project to a halt. The militia sent to defend the city used the church as a barracks and destroyed the pews to make room for the men. In 1780, during the British occupation of the city, the Redcoats also used the church as a barracks. They were no more kind with it than the American forces, resulting in even more structural damage. Once the war ended and repairs had been completed, the church was dedicated in 1787.

In 1817, thirty years after both the Meeting and Archdale Street buildings acting as one church, Anthony Forster, a Society minister, became a Unitarian. He took with him seventy-five members of the congregation, who helped establish the Archdale location, as the base of their church. In 1852, Francis D. Lee, a Charleston architect and church member, was hired to modernize the building, giving the church its first construction project since 1787. His inspiration for remodeling came from the Chapel of Henry VII at Westminster Abbey and St. George's Chapel at Windsor Castle. These styles can be seen in the church we know today.

A few years after construction was completed, a disaster nearly brought it all down. In 1861, the Great Charleston Fire swept through the city. In all, 560 acres of buildings were razed to the ground. In the countless buildings destroyed were many houses of God, including the Circular Congregational Church and the nearby Roman Catholic Cathedrals of St. John and St. Finbar. Either fortune or divine intervention held back the fire at the church's front door. Caroline Gilman writes: "Our fences burnt down and nothing was visible but burnt arches…but there stood our Church in all its beauty and our Cemetery with not a rose-bud crushed." No doubt the congregation felt like they had been saved by the hand of the Lord. Twenty-five years later, however, Unitarian's parishioners would be saying quite the opposite. The Charleston Earthquake of 1886 struck, shearing off the entire top of the church's tower. The earthquake left a massive hole in the church ceiling, and some rubble that had fallen into the churchyard caused more damage. The church was once again repaired, thanks to the cooperative effort of Unitarian churches across the nation.

The church may have a lot of good history, but you have come here to learn about its spooks. Rest assured, there are plenty of those to satisfy an appetite for the supernatural. The most famous specter of the church is a young woman named Anna Ravenel, who died sometime in 1827 at the age of fourteen. Her story begins with her meeting and falling in love with a young soldier stationed near Charleston.

The young man's name was Edgar Perry. Anna's father did not approve of the young man and had already promised her hand in marriage to a local wealthy businessman. Naturally, the father forbade her from seeing the soldier. Back then, with the exception of officers, a military man did not hold a high post in society. In fact, most servicemen were poor. Still, the unfavorable circumstances did not stop the two young lovers, who hatched a plan. In this plan, Anna would sneak out at night and meet Edgar at the Unitarian churchyard. There, among the dead, they could be with each other almost every night. The young couple got away with these encounters for some time before her father figured out his daughter was up to something. One night, he followed Anna as she met her lover at the church. After catching the couple together, Anna's father locked his daughter in her room and would not permit her to leave. Shortly after this, Edger was sent back to Virginia and Anna, who had contracted yellow fever, soon died from her ailment. The young girl was laid to rest in the family plot. Word eventually reached her former love interest, who made his way to Charleston to pay his final respects at her grave. When Anna's father learned about the soldier's return, he ordered all the graves to be dug up and then reburied in unmarked graves, thus giving all the graves a freshly dug look. When Edgar arrived at the family plot, he was unable to find the correct grave and had to leave without saying his final goodbye to his dead love. Anna's specter is said to haunt the churchyard where she and Edgar once met in secret. Her figure darts between the tombstones and the trees of the

The graves of the churchyard.

landscape. Seen wearing a simple dress, she still waits for her love. Sometimes, she appears misty and transparent, and is easily mistaken for a small patch of fog. Fog, however, does not move through the churchyard with purpose.

Interestingly, Edgar Perry was the pseudonym used by Edgar Allen Poe to join the army. Poe was stationed at Fort Moultrie in 1827 and often headed to Charleston. He was also from Virginia, and returned there once he left the army. At the end of his life, the last piece of writing he would have published was a poem called "Annabel Lee," which concerned the death of a fair young woman he loved. The most common view is that "Annabel" was about his late wife, Virginia, but many in Charleston say its true inspiration was none other than Anna Ravenel. The poem follows in its entirety:

Annabel Lee

It was many and many a year ago,
In a kingdom by the sea,
That a maiden there lived whom you may know
By the name of ANNABEL LEE;
And this maiden she lived with no other thought
Than to love and be loved by me.

I was a child and she was a child,
In this kingdom by the sea;
But we loved with a love that was more than love-
I and my Annabel Lee;
With a love that the winged seraphs of heaven
Coveted her and me.

And this was the reason that, long ago,
In this kingdom by the sea,
A wind blew out of a cloud, chilling
My beautiful Annabel Lee;
So that her highborn kinsman came
And bore her away from me,
To shut her up in a sepulcher
In this kingdom by the sea.

The angels, not half so happy in heaven,
Went envying her and me–
Yes!–that was the reason (as all men know,
In this kingdom by the sea)
That the wind came out of the cloud by night,
Chilling and killing my Annabel Lee.

But our love it was stronger by far than the love

Of those who were older than we–

Of many far wiser than we–

And neither the angels in heaven above,

Nor the demons down under the sea,

Can ever dissever my soul from the soul

Of the beautiful Annabel Lee.

For the moon never beams without bringing me dreams

Of the beautiful Annabel Lee;

And the stars never rise but I feel the bright eyes

Of the beautiful Annabel Lee;

And so, all the night-tide, I lie down by the side

Of my darling–my darling–my life and my bride,

In the sepulcher there by the sea,

In her tomb by the sounding sea.

Whomever this poem is about, it shares elements with the legend of the two lovers: the couple was young, Charleston was a major port and much like a kingdom, and forces did conspire to keep the lovers apart.

Another spook haunting the church is that of a woman who is also waiting for her love. Mary Bloomfield lived in Charleston over one hundred years ago and enjoyed a very happy marriage with her husband. One fateful day, the husband informed her he was heading to Boston for business, something he had done many times before. She wished him well and gave him a goodbye kiss. Unlike the other trips her husband had taken, this one seemed to last longer. The days turned to weeks, and the weeks into months without a single word from him. She knew that he would never leave her and was positive he would return to her one day. Mary's story says that she spent the remainder of her life waiting on his return. After her passing, she was laid to rest at the Unitarian church. Much like Anna, she is also said to wander the grounds waiting on her love. Because Mary appears as an older woman wearing a white dress, she is often called the Lady in White. Strange lights are sometimes seen in the cemetery at night, giving off an ethereal glow. It is anyone's guess where these lights come from — Anna or Mary — or maybe, just maybe, both ladies are responsible.

BATTERY CARRIAGE INN

CHARLESTON
SOUTH CAROLINA

Another nearby haunting takes place at the famous Battery Carriage Inn. The inn is said to be home to several specters who are so enamored with the place that they refuse to leave. One can only imagine the bill they must have racked up. The inn's history began when Samuel N. Stevens, a prosperous lender and a broker of crops, purchased the property at 20 South Battery in 1843. He held onto the property until he sold it to John Blacklock in 1859. Shortly after, Blacklock's new home would become front row to the beginning of the Civil War.

The sight of large artillery cannons sitting so close to where he slept was enough to send Blacklock packing. Through the years, the house went through various owners, including a Yankee businessman who, despite attempts to make friends in the city, found himself unwelcome. Following the Yankee, the next owner was

Andrew Simonds, a phosphate-mining businessman and founder of the First National Bank of South Carolina. The Simonds family has made the inn, still owned by Andrew's descendants, what it is today by giving it nearly every amenity one could ask for. Some of these amenities even include a ghost or two.

The inn's most famous specter has been around before Andrew Simond purchased the property, dating back to the Civil War. He haunts what is now Room 8. This spook is particularly harrowing to guests who have the misfortune of encountering him. Folks staying in the room will awaken to a terrifying sight: a headless torso standing in their room! As if his frightening appearance is not startling enough, he is said to make the room ice cold. It is almost as if his presence gives the entire room a sinister air. Besides chilling the room, he drives pure terror straight through one's bones. Moreover, he darkens in the room, which only adds to the malevolent mood. In 1993, a skeptical guest awoke to the headless ghost standing by his bed. The skeptic reported the entity taking labored breaths, standing motionlessly. Still, the guest found the courage to reach out to the headless man and managed to touch the coat he wore. According to the guest, the coat felt like burlap, similar to the dress a man from the Civil War era would have worn.

As soon as he made physical contact, the apparition vanished in a flash, leaving behind one frightened and confused man. Most of the staff is convinced that the headless torso is the ghost of a soldier killed in an ammunition explosion during the final days of the Civil War. When cleaning the room, the staff is often too scared to look over their shoulders, afraid they will see the headless ghoul standing behind them. Beyond appearing in the room, he is thought to be the cause of strange thuds, as well as faucets supposedly turned on by themselves.

A less terrifying entity of the inn is lovingly called "The Gentleman Ghost." Legend says he is the spirit of a sensitive, but suicidal, college student, who leapt to his death from the inn's roof decades ago. Because he likes to keep women company, many female guests have awoken to the sound of someone crawling in bed with them. When they look, however, all they see is the impression of someone on the bed. Of course, this sight is enough to scare anyone out of their wits: if the woman screams, the Gentleman Ghost will promptly exit through a built-in entertainment unit, where the original door used to stand. Outside of these good-willed, but forced bed entries, he never seems to do anything else. He will not make any odd noises or mess with electronics. Crawling into bed with women seems to satisfy him just fine. At least this much can be said with certainty — he lives up to his name. He always leaves the woman alone once she objects to him joining her in bed. Of course, that is probably not much consolation to a woman who just had quite a personal encounter with the supernatural.

Sumter after the siege.

THE FALLEN AT SUMTER

CHARLESTON
SOUTH CAROLINA

There are so many places I love to see every time I get the honor of visiting Charleston. It is a city resplendent with history. As an avid history buff, when I come to Charleston, there is a must see: Fort Sumter.

Despite being among the most important locations from American history, Fort Sumter currently seems unimpressive to the naked eye. It is now little more than crumbling walls, so it is easy to forget its relevance. In 1860, South Carolina had already been considering secession and the election of Abraham Lincoln, a candidate for the Abolitionist Republican party, sealed the deal. On December 20, 1860, South Carolina seceded, hoping for a peaceful separation. As we know now, this proved to be an empty hope. Before South Carolina officially left the Union, President Buchanan wanted to make sure a capable commander was in the state in the event the worst-case scenario happened. Major Robert Anderson, a well-respected officer originally sent to Fort Moultrie, was Buchanan's pick. Shortly after his arrival, the state seceded and Confederate forces demanded that Anderson and his men vacate the fort and return to federally-controlled land.

Despite being a Confederate sympathizer, Major Anderson did not have the authority to relinquish his command. He knew the Southern army's superior numbers could easily overrun Moultrie. Anderson decided Moultrie was a death trap, so he and his 150 men abandoned the fort and made for Sumter in the Charleston harbor.

Sumter had been built after the War of 1812 to defend the city from naval-based attacks, so it seemed like the best spot from which to defend. Named after Revolutionary War hero General Thomas Sumter, construction began in 1829. The structure remained unfinished in 1861, when the Civil War began. Buchanan's attempts to re-supply Sumter on January 9th by sending a ship, the *Star of the West*, loaded with men and guns, failed when batteries from Charleston fired on the ship, forcing it to abandon the mission. This left Sumter in a precarious situation, with dwindling morale and supplies.

On March 4th, Lincoln was sworn in as the 16th President of the United States and was immediately brought up to speed on the Sumter situation. Unlike Buchanan, he made his stance about the Southern secession very clear: zero tolerance. Newly-elected Confederate president Jefferson Davis sent delegates to Washington to meet with Lincoln. The delegates were authorized to offer to buy all federally-controlled forts in the CSA, but they were rebuffed and sent away. This put the Confederate government on edge.

Lincoln was aware of the severe need Anderson and his men had for basic supplies, so he commanded the U.S. Navy to deliver them to Sumter. Lincoln did not desire to be the one to start a war, so he sent word to South Carolina's governor, informing him of the shipment and assuring him no weapons or soldiers were aboard. He stated, "That if war is to be started, it will be them who fire the first shot." Despite this warning, the ships were fired upon, resulting in Sumter receiving no new supplies. Both sides knew war was inevitable.

Their waiting ended on April 11th, when Confederate general P.G.T. Beauregard (who was actually a student of Anderson's at West Point) sent three aides to Sumter to plead with Anderson to surrender and leave the Fort.

I am ordered by the government of the Confederate States to demand the evacuation of Fort Sumter. My aides, Colonel Chestnut and Captain Lee, are authorized to make such demand of you. All proper facilities will be afforded for the removal of yourself and command, together with company arms and property, and all private property, to any post in the United States, which you may select. The flag, which you have upheld so long and with so much fortitude, under the most trying circumstances, may be saluted by you on taking it down. Colonel Chestnut and Captain Lee will for a reasonable time, await your answer. I am, very respectfully your obedient servant. G. T. BEAUREGARD.

Anderson responded in kind words:

General: I have the honor to acknowledge the receipt of your communication demanding the evacuation of this fort, and to say, in reply thereto, that it is a demand with which I regret that my sense of honor, and of my obligations to my government, prevent my compliance. Thanking you for the fair, manly and courteous terms proposed, and for the high compliment paid me, I am, General, very respectfully, your obedient servant. ROBERT ANDERSON, Major, First Artillery, Commanding.

After his refusal to leave the fort and Lincoln's unwillingness to sell it, Jefferson grew tired of this stand-off and ordered Beauregard to take Sumter.

The bombardment started at 4:30 in the morning on April 12th, as shells rained down on the fort like rain. As Lincoln intended it, the South had fired the first shots of the war. At that time, all that was inside Sumter, besides Anderson, were nine officers, sixty-eight enlisted men, eight musicians, and forty-three construction workers who were still putting the finishing touches on the fort. Regardless, at daybreak, they returned fire. For thirty-four hours, a savage artillery onslaught flew across the bay, blowing away Sumter's walls piece by piece. The once tall and mighty walls started to look like piles of dust and rubble. A former Texas senator rowed out without permission to see if the garrison was trying to surrender. Anderson decided that with supplies and ammunition dwindling, his position was hopeless. Finally, he had a white flag raised over the fort to signal their surrender.

Surprisingly, not a single solider from either side died during the three-day siege (one Confederate horse died, however). The Confederacy did not want prisoners at this time, so they asked Anderson to take his men and leave. Maybe if Anderson had not asked to have a hundred-gun salute, all the Union defenders would have made it home alive. The fort's defenders were permitted to perform a hundred-gun salute as the American flag was lowered and the Confederate one took its place. The first forty-six cannons fired without a hitch, but the forty-seventh misfired, killing both men operating it and wounding four others. One of the men who died in the blast was Private Daniel Hough; born in Tipperary, Ireland, Hough emigrated to the United States around the 1840s. He was a regular in the army, which was not too common before the start of the Civil War because it was a low-paying job where you were not well treated; thus, this was not a big draw for young men of the day. He enlisted in 1859 and then re-enlisted in January 1861. He was assigned to Battery E of the first United States Artillery Regiment and stationed at Fort Sumter. Hough was buried at Sumter quickly after his death, while Confederate troops marched to the island and his comrades departed. Since his comrades interred his body, though, it seems Hough's spirit is anything but at rest there. After the war, Sumter served as an unmanned lighthouse from 1876 to 1897, so for nearly two decades it saw virtually nobody on the island. In 1898, the Spanish-American War started, and a new interest in Sumter as a military fort emerged.

The ghostly face in the flag.

As restoration took place on the island, workers claimed to smell gunpowder, even though no one had fired a shot on the premises in over thirty years. It was easy for this incident to be brushed aside as residue from the war lingering in the old bricks and walls, so not much thought was put into it. As years went by, though, not only did military personnel and civilians smell smoke, but they also heard the sounds of battle on the calmest nights and experienced strong emotions of sadness and fear that did not originate from their own hearts. Still, none of these experiences had as much effect as the smoky figure seen throughout the years.

Seen far too many times to be an illusion, the figure more often than not is described as having a human form seemingly made out of grey smoke, though he has also been seen as a black shadow figure. People normally saw him by the walls, standing at attention, but when anyone tries to approach…he disappears like a puff of smoke. People commonly believe this is the ghost of Hough; however, this theory is not conclusive. Though he was the first human casualty there, he was not the only man to die on its grounds during the war.

Major General Quincy A. Gillmore and Rear Admiral John A. Dahlgren, after bombarding Sumter, launched both a Naval and Army attack on September 8-9, 1863. Because the Navy and Army refused to work together, the attack was a disaster and the casualties were high. The Navy would continue attacks on the fort after this, and more and more men would die at Sumter. Therefore, with all that death, it is difficult to pinpoint who actually haunts Fort Sumter — it is possible it is just one man or more than one.

Hough, however, is the only candidate for the face on Sumter's flag — the very flag taken down during the 100-gun salute is said to have faded in such a way to produce a face on it. The face first appeared as the flag toured the country, after Sumter's fall, to raise support for the Union's war effort. People noticed that within the stars a face seemed to peer back at them and people who knew the late Daniel Hough claimed, undoubtedly, Hough's face gazed from the flag he had given his life to reclaim. The next time you are in Charleston, do yourself a favor and visit Sumter. I cannot promise that if you take the thirty-minute ferry ride to the island you will see its ghostly sentinel, but you just may feel his presence or smell the gunpowder from the battle. If nothing else, the fact you will be standing in the spot where the Civil War started makes it worth the trip!

The Headless Sentry

THE HEADLESS SENTRY

GEORGETOWN
SOUTH CAROLINA

The American Revolution has no shortage of bigger than life characters. As people, we are not above embellishing a good story to bring it to the level of myth and legends. Francis Marion, or more commonly the Swamp Fox, is one of the Revolution's more interesting figures. He did not sign the Declaration of Independence and there were no acts of valor or amazing feats in any huge battles (although he did fight in them) that made him famous. Instead, it was his numerous stealth attacks that brought him fame. Marion certainly helped the oppressed colonists gain their independence and long after his passing his legend inspired not only books, but also Mel Gibson's character in the movie *The Patriot*.

Born around 1732, on his family's plantation in Berkeley County, South Carolina, he was the youngest in his family, and is said to have been born with malformed legs. Like a seventeenth-century Theodore Roosevelt, Marion refused to let anything slow him down; at the age of fifteen, determined to make his own way, he started serving on a ship. However, fate had written a different story for him — and its prologue opened with disaster. The ship sank on its first voyage, supposedly brought down when a whale rammed into it. Luckily, the seven-person crew escaped on a lifeboat and, within a week, reached shore. Not surprisingly, this experience proved to Marion that staying on dry land would be best.

By the time Marion was twenty-five, the French and Indian War was starting. He joined the South Carolina Militia to fight the Cherokee and their French allies. Fighting the Cherokee provided lessons he would later use in battle; thus, ironically, it was his enemy who taught him the tactics that later served him against the British. He noticed that the Cherokee would attack from the woods, then quickly retreat — a strategy that dealt maximum damage to their enemies while minimizing their own losses.

Years later, as the fires of the Revolution were just igniting, he would become captain of one of three regiments raised by South Carolina. In this capacity, he spent the first few years primarily defending Fort Sullivan and then, one night in March 1780, an event transpired that would fortify his role in American history. Marion was attending a dinner party in Charleston. Marion, who abstained from alcohol, took his leave from the party of drinking men, but now he faced a problem: all the doors had been locked to prevent anyone from entering and ruining the toast. Marion needed to make haste and had no patience to wait for the end of the toast. Instead, he decided to exit from the second-floor window. In his attempt to climb down, he lost his hold and fell. To worsen matters, he had broken his ankle. Ultimately, the injury turned out to work towards his benefit, and, in turn, towards that of the American cause in the Revolution.

Knowing he would heal faster outside of Charleston, Marion left for the countryside. In turn, when Charleston fell to the British shortly after his injury, he was not there to become a prisoner. Marion, soon realizing conventional warfare would not aid them in defeating the British, taught his men the swift, crafty military skills he learned from the Cherokee. These fresh, new tactics would slow down the British advance. Marion displayed cunning in survival by hiding in the woods and making stealthy, quick attacks on his foes. Like a band of wanted thieves lurking in the woodlands, he and his men attacked with the speed and deadliness of a dagger. Marion eventually earned his nickname from British Lieutenant Colonel Banastre Tarleton, who had been informed of Marion's whereabouts by an escaped prisoner. Tarleton chased the American militia for seven grueling hours, covering some twenty-six miles. Marion finally eluded Tarleton in a swamp, leaving the Colonel angry and demoralized. "As for this damned old fox," said Tarleton, "the Devil himself could not catch him." The story spread rampantly, and soon the locals started cheering for "The Swamp Fox."

As the legend goes, The Swamp Fox took on a daring mission to save the father of one of his most trusted men. The British were holding him at the plantation owned by a man loyal to the British crown. Wounded American soldiers were also interned on the property, which made the rescue even more urgent.

Thankfully, patriotism still lived in the heart of the plantation owner's daughter. She defied her father and provided information to The Swamp Fox whenever she could. Further, she would leave messages for Marion at the graveyard of the nearby Prince George Church. She hid them in one of the tombs for him to visit and retrieve. Aware that the captured father was old and frail, Marion wished to rescue him soon, for he feared the man would relinquish valuable information under torture. The plantation owner's daughter helped by inviting all the soldiers stationed at the plantation to a dinner party at a neighboring estate. One sentry remained to guard the prisoners.

Meanwhile, Marion and a small group of his men crossed onto the property. The lone sentry did not stand a chance, and Marion's men showed no mercy. A swift sword removed the sentry's head, removing any opposition. The militiamen not only rescued the prisoners, but escaped without a single injury. However, the memory of that heroic rescue goes far beyond that night — farther even than the Revolution.

Soon after his death, the apparition of the headless British soldier was seen on the grounds. Even to this day, he will appear to wave his weapon at anyone who crosses his path, as if he is telling them to leave. Other times, one can see the sentry marching throughout the grounds, looking for his head. He eventually appeared so often that the plantation's servants began wearing crucifixes for protection, for they feared the ghost intended them ill will. Even though a golf course now covers most of the property, some people claim to see the headless apparition wandering the old grounds during the night. Unlike many other headless ghosts, the sentry never appears as a disembodied light, but a full-bodied apparition.

So, if you ever find yourself playing 18 holes in Georgetown and you see a man in a red uniform approaching you, don't be surprised if he is missing his head!

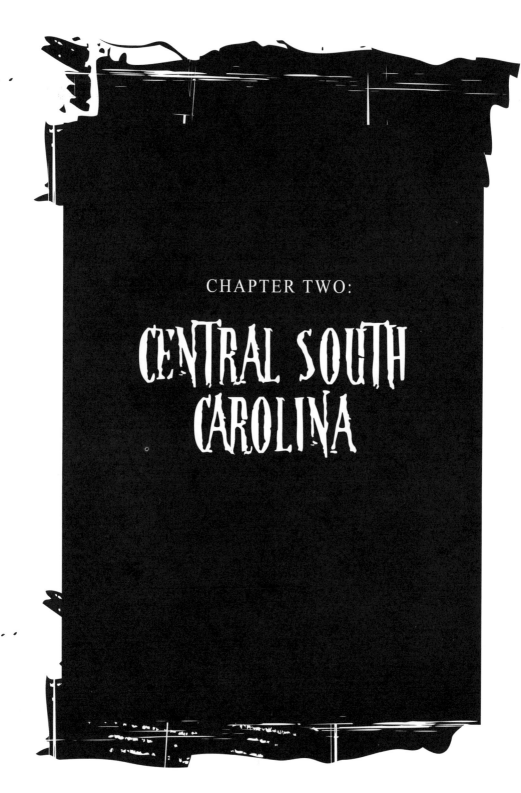

CHAPTER TWO:

CENTRAL SOUTH CAROLINA

The Third Eye Man

LEGEND OF THE THIRD-EYE MAN

COLUMBIA
SOUTH CAROLINA

At first, I debated this story's inclusion, as the Third-Eyed Man is not a ghost by any account. Whether or not it actually exists, this entity is something else entirely. I consider myself fairly open to supernatural experiences; I love visiting haunted houses or cemeteries where there have been reports of "shadow people." However, I do not want to see it firsthand and, after you read about it, I think you will agree.

The University of South Carolina, located in Columbia, was founded in 1801 as the College of South Carolina. During the Civil War, the college was closed and, similar to many other campuses at the time, turned into a military hospital for the war's duration. On May 24, 1865, Union forces occupied the campus; after the war, they returned it to the state and it was reopened as a college campus. Now, like in most cities, Columbia has an underground world, also known as the catacombs.

There are three sets of tunnels; some think they are all connected, though no evidence exists to validate this. One series rests under USC, a series runs under Columbia [the larger], and then a series under the Five Points area.

All spooky tunnels come with a scary story or two. The caverns beneath the university have their own brand of spooky tales. On the night of November 12, 1949, Christopher Nichols and a friend were walking near the Longstreet Theatre when they saw a strange man in the middle of the street. Chris first noticed that the man's clothes seemed made from the silvery shine in the night. Before either boy could get a better look, the oddly-dressed man lifted a nearby sewer lid and climbed down, sealing the lid behind him.

At the time, Chris worked as a reporter for the college paper, *The Gamecock*. He wrote a story entitled "The Sewer Man," in which he talked about his sighting of the man and his disappearing down a sewer hole. This created a stir with his fellow students, some of whom were panicked. After a while, no new sightings came and interest in the story died; this created the assumption that Chris had seen a homeless man or had fabricated the encounter in order to sell a story.

Six months later, another, even more credible witness came forward. On April 7, 1950, a university police officer out on patrol came face-to-face with the "Sewer Man." He discovered two mutilated chickens behind the Longstreet Theatre while out on patrol. Returning to his squad car, the officer reported the parts strewn all over the dock. Assuming it was a twisted fraternity prank, he returned to the scene, finding the silver muddled man huddled over the chicken pieces. He shined his flashlight on him to find a very disturbing face, grotesque in color and shape, and a third eye in the middle of his forehead staring back at him. He retreated from the scene and called for backup, with a little panic in his voice. When his fellow officers arrived, he took them to the spot, only to find a few feathers and chicken bones. Despite his continued attempts to convince them, he could not get anyone to believe he had seen what he reported to them.

After this, the creature became known as "The Third Eye Man" and students began descending into the underground to see if they could see this horror for themselves. Many claim to have seen him, but offer no proof. It is very possible they just want bragging rights. Somewhere circa 1960, nearly twenty years after the last substantial sighting, several fraternity brothers and three pledges descended into the catacombs beneath Gambrell Hall. The catacombs was a popular hangout for students and, until this point, nobody had been hurt. This night, however, the boys turned a corner and saw what they assumed was a crippled man covered in silver. When he turned to look at them, they saw he had a third eye and his face resembled something from a nightmare.

Before they could react, the beast grabbed a metal pipe and began attacking them. Matthew Tabor was struck and knocked to the ground, but was able to get back on his feet and leave the tunnel. The creature descended back into the darkness once the boys made a run for it; Matthew earned a few scratches and bruises that needed treatment after the tunnel incident. With a student injured, police launched a large search of the caverns, progressing with the understanding that they were looking for a deranged man, not some storybook monster. Even so, they never found anyone — man or monster.

Still, the university decided action had to be taken. They did not want any more students entering the catacombs and risking harm to themselves, so every access was sealed off and a warning was issued. If any student tried to gain access, they would face expulsion and all trespassers would face prosecution to the fullest extent of the law.

This is commonly seen as a way of preventing people from venturing into the maze of dark underground tunnels and risking injury, but others say that the school is aware that The Third Eye Man exists and is trying to seal him off in order to starve him to death. If he were a flesh and blood creature, he most certainly would have starved by now. Is it possible, though, that he found a way out of the catacombs? Reports of sightings have surfaced in the last three decades, and paranormal investigators have desperately tried to access the catacombs to check for themselves, but without permission from the university, it is relatively impossible.

Wade Hampton III as he looked among the land of the living.

THE GHOST RIDER OF COLUMBIA

COLUMBIA
SOUTH CAROLINA

I have met many former members of the armed service in my day. I have also been friends with a good deal of them. Not shockingly, then, I have never met any who are war fanatics; after all, they have seen it first-hand. They are often the ones who think it should be the absolute last resort for a people. They will often spend the rest of their lives preaching this, and in the case of the The Ghost Rider of Columbia, they will use the next life for it, too.

Wade Hampton III was born into a wealthy South Carolinian family and lived there all his life. His prominent family owned large plantations in both Mississippi and South Carolina. He spent his youth learning to ride horses, surviving in the wilderness, and, according to some stories, hunting bears with nothing more than a knife! When he got older, he received his formal education at South Carolina College (currently the University of South Carolina). Though he studied law, Wade never practiced it, opting instead to manage his family's plantation.

In 1858, upon his father's death, Wade inherited a vast fortune. Additionally, by the time the Civil War commenced, he managed to become a senator. Initially, he did not support South Carolina's decision to secede from the Union. However, once the state ratified it, he maintained loyalty to his home state, choosing to resign his senatorial seat. He went on to humbly enlist in the Confederate Army as a Private; however, despite having zero military experience, he was asked to take a commission as a Colonel instead. Little doubt exists his promotion was based on two facts: Wade had already established himself as a capable leader in the South, so serving as a Private would be somewhat beneath him; and secondly, his wealth permitted him to fund his troops, arming them and paying for necessities. In fact, he managed to exhaust the majority of his fortune on necessities.

Wade organized "Hampton's Legions," which consisted of six companies of infantry, four companies of cavalry, and one artillery battery. The "Legion" engaged the Union forces at the Battle of Bull Run in July 1861, where he managed to receive his first of four wartime injuries. Despite lacking military experience, he proved to be a very good commander and by the end of the war rose to Lieutenant General. Still, Wade witnessed the defeat of the South at Gettysburg and saw the Confederate war effort grow increasingly futile.

Though this was tragic by itself, Wade suffered a much greater personal tragedy while he served near Petersburg, Virginia. During the war, his sons, Thomas and Wade IV, served under him. He ordered Thomas to ride ahead, to deliver a message to fellow officers. Within the next two hours, Wade, along with his other son, followed Thomas down the same road. To their horror, the pair came across Thomas's body on the side of the road. When Wade IV dismounted to inspect his brother's body, someone fired upon him while his father watched. Wade managed to escape the ambush, but battled with deep sorrow and disbelief.

Despite losing his sons, Wade Hampton III remained loyal to and even continued fighting after Robert E. Lee's surrender at Appomattox Court House. In April of 1865, he finally surrendered, alongside Johnston, to General William T. Sherman in North Carolina. In the end, the war took everything from him: his wealth, his boys, and, when he returned home, he learned his home had burned to the ground in Sherman's march to the sea. Although bitter for a while after the war, he eventually moved on with his life and served as both Governor and Senator of South Carolina from 1879 to 1891. Wade was eighty-four years old when he passed away on April 11, 1902. Wade had become so beloved in Columbia that an estimated 20,000 mourners lined the street as his corpse was transported to Trinity Churchyard to be laid to rest. After his body was interred, Columbia's citizens assumed the man had been seen for the very last time.

Wade made a one-time appearance during the spring of 1914, twelve years after his death. A man rode a horse down one of Columbia's main roads. As this was a time when a car was still a novelty item, this was a relatively acceptable sight and might have gone unnoticed. Nevertheless, it did not go unheeded! Instead, it roused panic and alarm to anyone who saw him. Why was this "common" sight causing such panic? The answer is simple: the man rode his horse several feet off the ground! Shortly after making his appearance, the man vanished.

Naturally, people did not know what to make of this supernatural event. Some claimed it was a sign from God, while others believed they witnessed the arrival of one of the Horsemen of the Apocalypse, signifying the arrival of Judgment Day. Finally, one random witness realized it was Wade Hampton III. His face was well known to the people and once it was recognized the people had little doubt it was him…returned from the grave.

The story goes that a few months later, this event's importance became clear. Some folks believed that Wade's ride through Columbia served as an omen for World War I. Considering all he lost, it would make sense that he would have lost his taste for war and, in his afterlife, serve as a harbinger to warn the denizens of his beloved city. Therefore, if what they saw was true, those who mistook Wade for one of the Apocalypse's horsemen were right. After all, one of the horsemen is War. His ghost has never appeared again to the people of Columbia. It would seem that one time was enough to get his point across.

THE GHOST OF NEWBERRY

NEWBERRY
SOUTH CAROLINA

Newberry County has no shortage of spectral and otherworldly residents. They roam the bridges, schools, and cemeteries. We are going to hear about a few of them, but let's get the history out of the way first.

Newberry County was formed in 1785, shortly after the birth of the nation. Even before it became a county, it was the site of several Revolutionary War battles and helped give America its freedom. Additionally, it suffered General Sherman's wrath during his march to the sea, so it has somewhat of a bloody past.

Within Newberry County, and the appropriately named Newberry College (which is also found in the city of Newberry), there are stories of spectral occurrences. The Lutheran Church founded the college in 1856, originally intended as a seminary to train future ministers. Before long, though, it transitioned into a liberal arts school. During its earlier days, Newberry College prospered, except for the period during the Civil War when nearly all staff and students were called into service by the Confederate Army. Though temporarily shut down as an educational establishment, it served, at various times, as a field hospital for the Confederate and Union soldiers. It was not until 1877 that, with the help of the locals, the school returned to its proper function.

Newberry College is supposedly haunted by at least two spirits. Although odd activity is reported throughout the campus, it is Keller Hall's bell tower and Kinard Hall's second floor that seem to harbor the most recognized instances.

The tragic story of Madeline is known by every faculty member and student. The story goes that, at the end of the Civil War, a young Newberry resident met a Union solider stationed at the college. Naturally, this was not popular with the locals, who saw the Yankee Army as an occupying enemy. Madeline did not care — she wanted to be with him for the rest of her life.

The solider was transferred somewhere else, but promised that once the war ended he would return for her. That day never came. Shortly after he left, she received news that he had perished in battle. She was so overcome with grief that she committed suicide. According to the legend, she jumped from Keller Hall's bell tower, which is where people most often catch glimpses of her spirit today.

However, we should mention that Newberry College archivist Gordon Henry previously noted that Keller Hall was built in 1895 — many years after the Civil War. Unless the news of the soldier's passing took thirty years to reach Madeline, it is impossible that she jumped from there. Even so, she seems to have chosen that location to wander around and give students a fright. Madeline is seen looking down from the top of the bell tower, with an expression of sorrow written across her face. Others glimpse her walking by doorways or quickly darting upstairs. Sometimes people only hear a woman's sobs. Anyone brave enough to venture up to the bell towner find no one there...their arrival causes the sobs to stop, returning the world to silence. Despite the eeriness, she never seems to bear anyone ill-will; in fact, she does not seem to be aware of anyone's presence. I would hazard to say that this is fine with most people.

Kinard Hall's ghost is more of a troublemaker — it loves to turn faucets on, bang on walls, or open windows. Still, despite the mischievous nature of this unidentified entity, it appears to bear no ill-will towards anyone either.

Another strange occurrence happens in the Dufford Alumni Building. This turn-of-the-century Victorian mansion used to be a family home, but returned to the school a couple of years ago. Reports of curious events have come from the building. A refrigerator, sitting upstairs, is often unplugged, though nobody can figure out who unplugs it. The custodian notices this and though someone might assume it simply fell out, the plug looks like someone had pulled it from the wall and gently placed it on the ground. In addition to this, the spirit likes to walk around with loud footsteps and move chairs next to windows.

Whomever the college's entities might be, they seem very welcome. The faculty and students look forward to retelling Madeline's story every Halloween or attempting to discover the identity of the lost souls haunting their dorms.

The West End Cemetery houses some of Newberry's ghosts that are more pronounced. Unlike the ones at Newberry College, they are often more visible than heard. The most famous specter is "The Bride of the West End." Her story is very similar to that of Madeline's in that she was also engaged to a Confederate soldier slain in battle. In a fashion reminiscent of Romeo and Juliet, she chose suicide rather than lifelong separation from her ill-fated lover. Dressing in her wedding gown, the girl jumped from the balcony of her parent's home, killing herself. Ironically, death did not seem to reunite her, as she has been seen kneeling by a grave for over a hundred years. Additionally, witnesses have seen her roaming a nearby field. Sometimes, she is mistaken for a living person…until she disappears into a gray mist in front of them. Your average bride cannot do that. The most bizarre location attributed to her is a tree in the cemetery, where she sits to watch out for her fiancé.

There are reports of an old horse-drawn hearse seen on nights following a thunderstorm. The stygian-tinted horse pulling the hearse has eyes that glow red like hot coals; this strikes up a frightening image. Even when the hearse remains unseen, many people have heard the clip-clop of its horse hooves. People believe the nearby Boundary Elementary School rests over part of the cemetery. More specifically, the playground. Apparently, a lifeless entity took offense to this — more than one child was playing when a woman, garbed in black, appeared and yelled at them for being in the cemetery. She seems to stick around longer than the average apparition, remaining until they move a good distance from her. Who she was in life is unknown, but it seems she is unaware the school was built over that section.

Another local cemetery that is haunted is at Ebeneezer Church. However, there are no distraught war widows or angry custodians here; rather, its specter is of an altogether different breed, with reports of the Goshen hound having existed since before the Civil War. It is a large white dog the size of a St. Bernard. It appears to be a common hound dog and roams the grounds. The ghost hound of Goshen belonged to a traveling peddler, unjustly hanged for the murder of a local man in Maybinton sometime in the early 1800s. His loyal dog was unwilling to leave his master's side and stayed by his grave until his own death. This hound is still keeping guard around his master's grave to this day. People who enter the graveyard have claimed to be chased out by an ethereal guard dog. He will run alongside the car regardless of its speed. If they stop their vehicle, the hound will reappear directly in front of the automobile. Finally, the pooch has been seen up to five miles, in any direction, from the old church, chasing cars and people, as would a living animal.

THE PARTYCRASHING SPECTER

CAMDEN
SOUTH CAROLINA

Most everyone I know enjoys a good party now and then. It's just good fun! Depending on the party, one can find people of all different ages. At Cool Springs Plantation, where some parties of the past never end, there are people in their twenties, fifties, and seventies — and not all of them are among the living. Cool Springs was built some time before 1832. Among the people who owned the massive home was a man named Dixie Boykin, who, by all accounts, enjoyed a good party when he was among the living. The details of his life's departure are somewhat debatable; some say his hard-partying ways did him in, while others think he was murdered in coldblood. His tale goes something like this.

Late one evening, Dixie had what appeared to be a heart attack in front of his young daughter. He urged her to go and retrieve his medicine from his room. She immediately rushed from her father's side. When she was near his bedroom, she ran into her stepmother, who told the girl she was too panicked and her behavior would do more harm to her father. The stepmother told the young girl to go and rest upstairs, assuring her she would not only take care of her father, but everything would be all right. She lied; just twenty minutes later, the young girl's father died.

Some have suggested that the stepmother killed Dixie, citing that she forbade Dixie's children from attending his funeral. Moreover, Dixie was the woman's third husband to die of "accidental" death. Now, of course, there was no proof she actually murdered her husband; after all, if he was having a heart attack, it is extremely unlikely that any medicine in the home would have helped him. Still, to this day, most people will claim he was murdered. The method? Poisoned by his wife, who would not allow his daughter to interfere with her scheme to claim his fortune for her own. It is possible that Dixie shares this view as well; reports say his spirit still haunts his former home, but unlike most spooks, he does not stomp around in the dead of night — rather, he walks about when the house is packed with guests.

John Bonner, a former Curator of Rare Books at the University of Georgia, purchased the home after its long vacancy. Bonner put years into reconstructing the plantation. He ultimately transformed it from a nearly dilapidated structure to its original prestige. Maybe the restoration stirred up the spirit said to inhabit the place. Seeing his former home brought back from the brink of death may have put Dixie into a celebratory mood — and celebrate is exactly what he loves to do. Every party thrown at the plantation is reported to have at least one uninvited guest, although in Dixie's view he is welcome by default. Encounters normally go like this:

> In a large social gathering, as the guests enjoy their drinks and listen to the music, someone will notice a man walking through the room. The mystery man, dressed in garbs of another time, seems to pay no mind to those around him, and those he walks near do not seem to notice him at all. Others have claimed to seen him walk right through closed doors, completely unfazed by matter. It has even been reported he is not above drinking someone else's beverage. Whenever a full wine glass or something of that kind is left unattended, it is later found empty by the one who set it down. It is customary for residents and guests of the house to leave a glass of champagne sitting out for Dixie in case he gets thirsty.

Dixie is thought to be responsible for the early 1900s music sometimes heard in the house. Most people figure that he does not like to wait for the owners to throw a shindig, so he takes it upon himself to initiate a party. No one can tell where the music comes from, but they know it is not of this era. The melodies echo down the halls of the house, and no matter where you look for the source of it, the music always sounds like it is a few rooms away.

Sightings of Dixie are rare these days. The music, too, is seldom heard. I do not know if he still likes to drink the champagne left out for him. Maybe Dixie has finally had enough of the party scene and is ready to pack it in and retire. You never know, it's possible!

Agnes's final resting place.

AGNES OF GLASGOW

CAMDEN, SOUTH CAROLINA

Many of us have at least once in our lives claimed to be so in love with another we would follow them to the ends of the earth. Not saying I have myself, but I have known a few. With most of us, though, this turns out to be idle talk — this was not the case for a young woman named Agnes.

One of South Carolina's most notable tales is that of Agnes of Glasgow. Agnes was a young woman who seemed only to come to America so she could die at the age of twenty. Agnes was born in Glasgow, Scotland, and it was there she met and fell in love with Lieutenant Angus McPherson, a British officer. The lovers supposedly had undying devotion to each other and eventually were engaged. However, shortly after their engagement, war in the American colonies broke out and McPherson left to fight.

Naturally, Agnes was distraught and, despite no known documentation of when he actually shipped out, her patience ended around 1779. She managed to sneak aboard a British vessel bound for Charleston; its cargo was troops and supplies. Shockingly, she made the entire voyage without discovery (women were considered bad luck aboard ships back then).

Once she arrived in the strange new world, Agnes started searching for her beloved. It is not known how many people she questioned, as well as how many towns and villages she wandered to before she located someone who knew of McPherson. When she finally did find someone, the person directed her to Camden, which at that time was a backwoods town not easily gotten to. Considering there was a war going on, her difficulty grew exponentially.

Through no small effort, she reached Camden, but the journey took a terrible toll on her. Sick and weakened by her journey, Agnes nevertheless arrived in Camden with a hopeful heart. Tragically, she quickly learned her love either had already moved on or had never been there at all. The news devastated her. With this newest heartbreak and her illness worsening, Agnes died far from home in Camden in 1780. Folklore lends that she was buried, under the cover of darkness, in Camden by King Haigler of the Wateree Indian tribe. This story is suspect since the Shawnee tribe reportedly slayed him on August 30, 1763. Regardless of who buried her, Agnes's grave is very real in the Quaker Cemetery in Camden and is visited by anyone interested in the legend.

Since Agnes's death, people have spoken of seeing a young woman roaming near the cemetery. If it is Agnes, she continues the search for McPherson. Cemetery visitors have even said they heard a Scottish woman asking, "Have you seen him?", only to look around for the lass and see no one around. Next time you are in Camden, make sure to stop by and pay your respects to Agnes of Glasgow. Maybe you will hear a sweet Scottish voice asking you, "Have you seen him?"

CHAPTER THREE

PIEDMONT SOUTH CAROLINA

THE INN AT MERRIDUN

UNION
SOUTH CAROLINA

The Merridun Inn could be torn right out of a page of southern history. Shady oaks and centuries-old magnolias surround it, so it comes as little surprise that it is on the National Register of Historic Places. The nine-acre property is just secluded enough to allow any visitor to feel like they have stepped back in time.

Originally built between 1855 and 1857 by local merchant William Keenan, the property initially consisted of 4,000 acres and was known as the Keenan Plantation. Benjamin H. Rice, a local Union lawyer, acquired the house and property in 1876. He had inherited a plantation in the Buffalo area, known as Pleasant Grove, which adjoined the Keenan property. At the time of purchase, the house in Union became the town home on this now 8,000-acre estate, where cotton was the main industry. Later, in the early 1880s, the home received some major renovations. Eventually, T. C. Duncan acquired the place and remodeled his new home in the Georgian classic revival style. The original, plain double piazzas with Doric columns were replaced with Corinthian columns. Duncan also added side wing marble porticos, resulting in over 2,400 square feet of porch space. These were only a few of Duncan's additions.

No longer a plantation or simple family home, Merridun is a place for travelers to hang their hats and maybe meet a friendly, sometimes playful spook. Supposedly, the inn is home to ten human spirits and one white dog that belongs to a red-headed ghost. Curious folks have glimpsed the spirits of Native Americans and former owners roaming the grounds. Visitors have reported seeing the entities walking by open doors or upstairs. Though visually detected at times, more often they have been heard, felt, and even smelled.

It is not uncommon to be taken by the overpowering scent of cigar smoke in some rooms. The experience is alarmingly real; visitors report feeling the smoke blowing in their faces. Anyone who has ever been near cigar smoke knows the smell cannot be missed. One particular specter seems to have a more pleasant aroma — that of fresh-cut roses. Perhaps this specter, bothered by cigar smoke, is trying to cover up the scent.

For many years, the inn had a mascot — JD the cat, an orange tabby who greeted all the guests and loved the attention they gave him. He passed away in 2008. The inn's staff and guests grieved for the loss, but fortunately, they will always have the memories of JD, including his own dealings with the paranormal. One could often see JD staring at things invisible to the human eye. It is not uncommon for animals to see the unseen in haunted homes, but in JD's case, the phenomenon went a little further. The tabby sometimes occupied empty rooms and seemingly stared at nothing; then he would meow towards empty air and move his head as if someone were doing a trick for him. He also got along fine with the ethereal white dog frequently seen in the home. At times, however, the white pooch got JD blamed for things he was not responsible for. Considering the tabby's behavior, one has to wonder if JD was truly alone when he laid by the window in the sun.

On one occasion, a group of guests had been downstairs learning about the history of the home. Meanwhile, JD basked in the attention as he laid by the window to take in some sunlight. Soon the inn's tour leader led the group to the second floor to see their rooms. During the tour, one man felt an animal dart by him and brush against his leg, almost causing him to lose his balance. He told the tour leader that the cat almost knocked him over. The guide told him that JD never goes upstairs. Sure enough, when the man went back to check, the cat was still perched by the window. Interestingly, the feeling of a small animal jumping on their bed has awakened many guests, but by the time they turn on the lights, they find no such creature in their rooms. Because the doors remain tightly closed, it is impossible for any living animal to gain entry. The white dog's ghost is believed to be responsible for these phantom encounters. He is also heard barking and, on rare occasions, whimpering in empty hallways and rooms. Guests will see him casually walking around the hallway, so they often mistake him for a living hound looking for someone to pet him.

A more human specter sometimes gives folks a startle late at night in their rooms. One night, a couple staying at the inn awoke to the covers being yanked off their bed. At first, they thought their bed sheets had snagged on something, so the couple simply pulled the covers back up. However, as soon as they laid back down, the covers once again came off.

Bed sheets, though, are not the only things that Merriidun's ghosts turn into playthings. Specters are known to disturb electronics. In fact, on one occasion, the inn's not-so-living residents refused to let a young woman's CD player work inside the house. Her player would work fine up to the front porch, but once she entered the building it would start skipping. Sure enough, as soon she stepped back outside, it would function normally. Perhaps some of the ghosts simply did not share her taste in music.

Whether it be a friendly, playful dog barking in the bedroom or a long-dead woman walking upstairs, the haunts at Merridun may be mischievous, but they are never menacing for those who choose to spend an evening there.

The Snow House.

THE SNOW HOUSE

SANTEE
SOUTH CAROLINA

When I first started working on this book, a good friend of mine named Doug Bridges urged me to contact his sister Betty. He informed me that she and her husband owned a historic house in Santee, South Carolina, which was full of unworldly activity. I soon got in contact with Betty, who was more than glad to give me the rundown on her haunted home. It was constructed in 1828 in Orangeburg, South Carolina. During the Civil War, it was used as an infirmary by the Confederate Army and would later be spared the torch during Sherman's march to the sea because a Northerner was in the home at the time. One of its former owners, Reverend Snow, actually moved the house to its current location on Lake Marion in Santee. In 1994, Betty and her family purchased the home, although they would not permanently move into it until 1999. In the years before this, it served as a lovely vacation home. Soon after they started getting to know the neighbors, they were informed that their new house had a few stories attached to it. One of the most interesting tales took place during the time Reverend Snow owned the house.

When Reverend Snow lived in the home, he had a friend house-sit while he was away. The main reason for the house-sitting concerned the care of his pet cat. The Reverend warned the guest not to be alarmed at night if the piano started playing, as his cat often ran across the keys. That night, the house-sitter awoke to the sound of the piano keys being smashed. Initially startled, he remembered what he had been told and fell back to sleep with ease. When he awoke the next morning, he looked for the cat so he could feed him. Although he looked from one end of the house to the other, he could not find the cat. Finally, he located the elusive feline outside…but the house-sitter remembered he had never let the cat back in before he went to sleep the night before. Confused, he told Reverend Snow about the weird events. Both men were at a complete loss as to how to explain what had happened. Betty said this story was confirmed by Reverend Snow himself, when they were introduced to him at the funeral of a friend of theirs.

Before Betty and her family moved in permanently, they allowed their friend to live there. The friend held a job in Kingstree as a schoolteacher. Betty told her she could stay there as long as she did some upkeep on the house and yard, as well as pay the utility bill. This was a larger undertaking than it sounds, for the home is large and the bill could be extremely high. As a result, Betty's friend spent almost all her time in the library of the house. Every night before she retired, she would make sure every light and appliance was off to save every penny. Some mornings, though, she would awaken to find the dining room light was on, the kitchen radio playing, and other strange instances of active electricity. One evening, one of the schoolteacher's friends spent the night. That friend would later tell her that she awoke in the middle of the night to find a dark, shadowy figure standing at the foot of the bed. The apparition made no move towards her and did not harm her, but waking up to such a sight would rattle anyone.

The schoolteacher was not the last to have a supernatural encounter. Betty's son had his own experience. He was in junior high at the time. Her son brought a friend with him on one of their vacation trips to the home. He and his friend slept in the library of the home, which at that time had bunk beds and a couch. In truth, it was more of a TV room. In the middle of the night, the friend came and woke Betty up and told her he was scared. He had been awakened by the feeling of something pelting him. The friend had been sleeping on the couch, and Betty's son on the bunk bed. The friend thought it was Betty's son goofing around, so he had kept telling him to stop. When the pelting persisted, he ran and got Betty, who said that when they turned on the lights…her son was sound asleep, but there were candy kisses (formerly sitting in a bowl on the coffee table) all over the couch! Both boys ended up sleeping in the parents' room that night and each night after for the duration of the trip.

Betty's husband also had a run-in with the supernatural. Once, he traveled alone to the house to enjoy some fishing. No point in having property on such a nice lake if one is not going to fish. Betty was in their Pennsylvania home at the time. One evening, she was speaking to her husband when he suddenly stopped mid-sentence and told her, "Someone is here with me." He could hear the distinct sound of someone walking down the hall towards his room. Betty's husband called out and asked who was in his house. Though no one responded, the footsteps continued down the hall. Her husband left his room, turned on every light in the house, and searched every room for the intruder. After his search, he discovered he was alone once more.

According to Betty, many others have gotten up in the middle of the night and packed their bags to go to a hotel due to hearing music, voices, or creaking sounds. As to who or what exactly haunts the home, there is no clear answer. The house did serve as a military hospital for a time, so it is very well possible that patients died there. Despite some renovations and added modern conveniences, much of the original structure still exists, such as the floorboards and windows. Maybe some specters from that era are just stopping by because it makes them feel at home.

The Old Bridge has seen better days.

CRYBABY BRIDGE

ANDERSON
SOUTH CAROLINA

In 1919, the bridge on High Shoals Road in Anderson — an approximately 194-foot-long, seventeen-foot-wide structure known as Crybaby Bridge — was built in Virginia and transported to Charleston. It was not until 1952 that people brought it to Anderson, South Carolina, where it replaced the older bridge.

Locals have a legend about this old bridge. The basic story involves a mother and child being killed in a tragic accident. Some people interject that the mother lost control of her car and drove off the side of the bridge. Others say they were walking on the bridge when a passing vehicle struck them; due to the darkness, the driver could not see them. As is common with most stories passed down by word of mouth, there is no shortage of variations.

The only thing everyone seems to agree on is the strange events that occur on the bridge at night. If you find yourself on the bridge (especially during a full moon), you supposedly will hear the disembodied sound of a baby crying. No matter how thoroughly you investigate, you will never be able to discern where the sound originates. Some people believe that provoking the spirits will garner a better reaction, but personally I always discourage this tactic. If something is haunting the bridge, it is a risky thing to make it have a grudge against you. Plus, it's rude.

One of the most common tales revolves around a phantom car that will slowly drive by. Witnesses describe it as a large black 1950s-era car. It will materialize from the darkness, its headlights giving off an eerie glow, and then it will soundlessly drive by before disappearing into the inky darkness from which it came. Some people suspect this is the woman's car from the night they died and they are replaying the events of their death…or, if the other version is correct, it could be the one that struck them.

This spot has become somewhat popular with local youths wishing for a cheap scare. They sneak out to the bridge in the dead of night to see if they can hear the ghostly infant making its heartbreaking and nerve-rattling cries. While doing this, some young adventurers have claimed to discover another phenomenon on the bridge — automobiles will often cut off for no reason, leaving the scared travelers stranded. No matter what is attempted, the cars will not start! One older gentleman, who worked as a mechanic most of his life, tried everything he knew to get his car running, but could not find a single problem with it. Finally, when he admitted defeat, his car started, which was even freakier for him because no one was in it at the time.

Why the ghost of the bridge likes to mess with cars is anyone's guess, but if I had to take a stab at it, I would imagine she does it to let people know she does not like being bothered. Although it is not that common, several people have claimed to see the mother's ghost. People approaching the bridge claim to see what at first appears to be a gray mist on the bridge. As they get closer, they notice it takes the form of a person in a dress, although no face is discernible. There are claims it looks as if she is holding something; most assume it is her child. Before anyone can draw near (if they have the nerve to try), the mist suddenly fades, often followed by the sound of an infant's crying.

The mother's identity, as well as her infant's, is unknown, as well as whether or not she truly ever existed. No evidence supports the claims there was an accident at the bridge. Additionally, we must also take into account the commonality of the story — most places have their own "Crybaby Bridge" that includes very similar elements. Still, the lack of documentation offers little to no concern for those who want to check out the bridge and have themselves a scary good time.

The former jail, which is now said to be home to spirits.

THE JAILHOUSE GHOST

PICKENS COUNTY
SOUTH CAROLINA

Located on the corner of Highway 178 and Johnson Street in downtown Pickens, the Pickens County Museum of Art and History once served as the county jail. Built in 1902, the castle-like building served as the jail until 1975. In 1944, American soldiers were still fighting Nazis in Europe, while racism was being fought here on the home front.

A cabbie, whose name was Johnny, picked up a young black man. Johnny was a diehard bigot, so it is probable he only picked up the young man so he could berate him with racial slurs and hateful jokes for his own sick amusement. For the ride's duration, the driver let loose a barrage of racist remarks, but his passenger never uttered a word, no doubt knowing any response would only egg him on.

When they arrived at the man's destination, the black man quietly departed the cab and started to walk away. Angrily, the cabbie jumped from his car, yelled that he had not received payment, and started chasing the young man down. The black man told him he refused to pay the fare because of the abuse he received during the ride before turning to walk away once more. Enraged, the driver ran back to his car and removed a gun. He immediately shot the offended passenger in the back, killing him.

Afterward, Johnny bragged about the killing. He took pleasure in the fact he had killed the black man because he had refused to pay the fare. Ironically, despite all his boasting, the police never arrested Johnny, choosing instead to cast a blind eye to his horrific actions. Racial tensions hit an all-time high after this. The black community was horrified that someone could be murdered without anyone being arrested, especially considering the culprit was proudly boasting about it whenever he got the chance.

It was during this time that Willie Earle came to visit his mother. At some point, she left him in the house because she needed to head to work. Sometime later that day, while she was working at the diner, she was confronted by a police officer, informing her that Willie had been arrested for robbing and stabbing a cab driver. Naturally, she broke down, refusing to believe her son could do such a thing.

Authorities took Willie to the Pickens County jail, but instead of getting a fair trial by his peers he would receive the harsh treatment of lynch mob mentality. A mob comprised of cab drivers entered the jail and forcibly took Willie to the old slaughter yard, where he was tortured and finally shot twice in the head. During this incident, no attempt was made by the police to prevent it. The cabbie who had been stabbed was Johnny, and he was the only one who went to work the next morning, acting as if nothing had happened. On February 21, 1947, thirty-one cab drivers were arrested for Willie Earle's murder, but in May, they were acquitted.

Willie never received justice for his brazen murder, and with the addition of his death's violent nature, it has led to Willie sticking around. Soon after his death, people would hear a phantom voice screaming, "I'm innocent, I didn't do it!" Even "guests" of the jail would become unnerved in their cells, feeling as if they were not alone. Long after the building ceased to operate as a jail, the phantom could still be heard professing his innocence to anyone who would listen.

Another of the jail's ghostly residents is the specter of a woman named Sarah.

The first sheriff to occupy the Pickens County jail was Sheriff James Henry Grace McDaniel. Back in the early twentieth century, it was not an uncommon practice to have a sheriff and his entire family live in the jailhouse. It seems that Sheriff McDaniel and his lovely wife Sarah had thirteen kids; the older boys were deputies while the older girls helped run the house with their mom.

With all the older kids doing chores and helping to keep the streets clean, the younger kids would play in the yard, as children are wont to do. A kitchen was built upstairs; Sarah spent a good amount of time there. She would periodically look out the upstairs window to make sure her kids were not getting into too much trouble and playing responsibly.

Sewage pipes, a relatively new invention at the time, were installed into the jail, but unfortunately, they were not installed correctly. The pipes started leaking into the well water, which did not bode well for the sheriff's family, as Sarah and five others developed Typhoid (typhoid fever is a bacterial infection of the intestinal tract and occasionally the bloodstream). The family suffered fevers, headaches, constipation or diarrhea, rose-colored spots on the trunk, and an enlarged spleen and liver. With modern treatment, the family would have most likely made a full recovery. However, medical science had not progressed to its current state and Sarah, her oldest daughter, and her oldest son's wife all succumbed to the disease.

Despite death cutting her ties to mortality, Sarah was not ready to leave the rest of her family behind. Shortly after her death, people started seeing Sarah's ghostly face; she was seen peering down from the second-story window. Perhaps she finds herself trapped in time and when she looks out that window, instead of seeing a modern town, she sees her children, still playing in the yard. To this day, she is said to still be there, watching from her window.

Whenever a cup or keys get moved, it is often thought it is Sarah keeping her home tidy. She is always welcome to those who witness her, as she is considered a loving and kind spirit…if not a somewhat somber one.

THE PLAY-LOVING GHOST

ABBEVILLE
SOUTH CAROLINA

I have always had a mild fascination with live theater. There is something thrilling about watching the people perform the scene live. I have seen my fair share of live performances, from productions of *A Christmas Carol* in large, ultra-modern theaters to small, independent plays in tiny, old bars converted for theater. The latter case can be seen in Abbeville, South Carolina, where the historic opera house is a town treasure to both the living and the dead!

The Abbeville Opera House has been in business for over a hundred years. Around 1908, a group of locals came up with the idea of constructing a stage for plays. The stage would serve well in Abbeville, which had become somewhat of an overnight stop for traveling productions moving from New York to places like

Atlanta. It seemed only logical, then, to sponsor a couple of these plays and give them a spot to perform in their town.

The Opera House paid off for the town right away, opening its residents to not only the best that Broadway had to offer, but also vaudeville, concerts, and eventually cinema (or "moving pictures" as they called them then). For a while, the building served both cinema and live theater, despite some people's belief that moving pictures were too lowbrow for the Opera House. Still, as always, technology kept progressing, and in 1927 *The Jazz Singer*, the very first "talkie," was released, changing the landscape of live theater. From there, the number of traveling productions declined drastically. The entire world stood in awe of these new films, complete with talking characters. Folks no longer cared to see stories done live. As expected, the Opera House became simply a cinema until its doors closed in the 1950s. Many thought the Opera House would be closed for good.

At this same time, a group that would eventually become the Opera House's savior was forming. This group, composed of lovers of the performing arts, was determined to preserve live theater in Upstate South Carolina. Known as A.C.T. (Abbeville Community Theater), they would perform in the old Chestnut Street School for their first decade. At some point, however, they decided to save the old opera house and use it for their productions. A.C.T. had their work cut out for them; they had to acquire a building that had been abandoned for over a decade. Fortunately, with the help of support in the town, they made it happen. On May 1, 1968, they performed their first Opera House play, which they fittingly called *Our Town*. The play featured a great deal about the dead who still hung around.

Theaters and ghost stories generally go hand-in-hand. As familiar as I am with ghost stories, even I have trouble thinking of a single theater over fifty years old that is not haunted. Heck, when I was in high school, people used to tell me the small, two-screen theater in town was haunted by the ghost of the old projectionist. The projectionist died of a heart attack decades before. Though no one claimed to believe it was true (although we did later find out the first projectionist did die, just not in the building), staff members were hesitant to go into the projection booth by themselves. As for the Opera House, people say it is haunted on the second-floor balcony, which was originally for the non-white patrons.

Nowadays, the old balcony of the Opera House is used for tech crews and equipment, lighting, and such. However, one single chair remains there — not for the crew, but for one particular audience member who is determined to have her seat. If a staff member moved the chair, the production would run into numerous problems, including lighting failures, curtain malfunctions, and other general technical issues. Eventually, the staff decided that the chair should remain untouched to avoid problems. The specter of the old Opera House is said to be a woman garbed in Victorian clothing. Actors, crew, and patrons of the theater have sighted her.

Occasionally, a performer has looked up at the balcony in the middle of their scene to see a woman watching them from the above. Doubtlessly, this ghostly sighting provided enough of a startle to make actors forget their next line. Because the second balcony is supposed to be vacant, staff will go up and inspect the area. Their natural suspicions tell them that someone must have snuck up to the balcony to watch the show free of charge, but no one is ever found. Moreover, it would be hard for a woman in such a cumbersome dress to get up there without being noticed.

It is not uncommon during a rehearsal, when the theater is nearly deserted, that after the end of a scene, claps can be heard from the empty chair. Frightened or not, the actors must also be flattered that they performed well enough for an invisible spectator. Besides clapping, talking can also be heard from up there. On the plus side, the woman never makes noises while a show is on, proving that at least she has good manners.

Several stories about the identity of this ethereal theatergoer float around. One tells of an actress who died in the theater after her performance in the 1920s. Another, more tragic tale is that of an African-American man who watched a play from the segregated booth and fell in love with one of the actresses when he saw her on-stage. However, the actress was white and, in those extremely intolerant times, interracial couples were nearly impossible. Regardless, he shared his feelings with her. In turn, she also developed feelings for him; despite the risk, they began seeing each other secretly. For a while, their relationship worked out and their love grew even stronger.

Eventually, though, word got out about this couple and an angry mob of white men formed to take action. The men waited for the play to start, knowing that the young man would be in the booth to watch the woman he loved. There, in the booth, they attacked. Some say they hanged him, others say the mob beat him to death. In despair, the young actress blamed herself for his death. Now that she has joined him in the grave, she sits in the booth with him. It is speculated that the chatter often heard from the balcony comes from the two lovers who no longer have to fear the racism of others. I personally hope that the second story is the right one; although the man died tragically, the couple can now be with each other in death!

Psychics who have visited the site say that the number of ghosts who haunt the theater reach up to at least a baker's dozen. It would seem that the other specters are not as vocal as the woman in the old balcony.

AFTERWORD

The places you have read about are just a few that South Carolina has to offer. Here are a couple more locations that are quite worth reading about and checking out if you get the opportunity.

HELLS GATE

SPARTANBURG
SOUTH CAROLINA

Oakwood Cemetery is known as one of the state's most haunted locations. It is a common tramping ground for paranormal investigators, both amateur and professionals alike. Amongst the surreal events people experience, are the loss of power to all electronics — phones, cameras, and flashlights all become useless. Children's laughter is often heard from behind gravestones, not to mention people endure the sensation of being tapped on the legs.

For the most part, the cemetery's spirits are harmless. They never do anything that will cause an individual permanent harm. However, this is not a location I would advise going to at night. Local police have had problems with people performing satanic rituals and there have been reports of grave-robbing. So if you decide to visit this location, make sure to only go during the day and bring a few friends with you.

THE BLOODY FLOORBOARDS OF BROOK GREEN

GEORGETOWN
SOUTH CAROLINA

Brookgreen Plantation was one of the largest rice plantations in the state in the mid-1800s. Although the property was owned by Josh and Bess Ward, its success was largely placed on the shoulders of a very cruel and sadistic man known as Fraser, the Ward's overseer, who ruled with an iron fist. He would take a slave he perceived as lazy and tie the man or woman to the barn floor and beat them near the point of death. All these beatings stained the barn's floorboards a dark and sickening red.

One of the house slaves, a young woman trusted by the family, was convinced to inform the Wards of Fraser's treatment of the slaves. By the time she worked up the courage to do so, the Ward's left the state to visit friends in North Carolina. Upon their return, the slave did not tell about Fraser's abusiveness. Fear of the man halted her from informing, and so the beatings continued up until the Civil War and the slaves were set free. Fraser had vanished from the plantation in the final days of the war; despite a large manhunt, the former slaves never found him, so they could not exact their revenge.

Long after the war ended, the floorboards of the old barn remained stained with the slaves' blood. Many attempts to paint over it or clean it up were made, but efforts did no good — the blood stayed on the floor until the 1930s, when the plantation was bought by Archer Huntington. He had the old barn town down, partly due to its morbid past. Although the barn and bloodstains are long gone, some folks still claim to hear the sound of some poor soul being whipped by Fraser's cold-blooded hand where the barn stood.

WIGG BARNWELL HOUSE

BEAUFORT
SOUTH CAROLINA

This home, now located at 501 King Street in downtown Beaufort, is not where it was originally constructed. The Wigg Barnwell House was constructed on the corner of Prince and Scott streets in 1816. The home had the dubious honor of serving as a hospital for the Union Army during the Civil War — serving as a Civil War hospital always seems to leave some form of scar on the property, and this one is no exception. Although the Civil War spirits have caused a few incidents there (sightings, moans, and moving objects), they have nothing on the ghost simply called "The Unwelcoming Spirit."

In the 1900s, the home was converted into apartments, as turning large houses into apartments was very common in those days. It is said that a young girl lived in one of the apartments; she was unmarried and lived by herself. It seems this made her a tempting target for some person wishing her ill will. Whoever this scoundrel was somehow tricked the girl into letting her in her apartment…and she was brutally murdered by the intruder. It was said to be a gruesome sight to behold the next day. Although an attempt was made to solve the murder, the lack of evidence and witnesses made it impossible.

After a time, the people of Beaufort pushed the murder to the back of their minds and went on with their lives. However, the people of the house she used to call home did not…because she wouldn't let them. Since her death, the spirit of the girl has made sure her presence is never forgotten. She has scared the daylights out of people for over a hundred years: tossing objects, making slamming noises against walls, and now and then appearing in the dead of night. It is suspected that she will haunt the house until her murder is solved, but if it was nearly impossible then, it must be completely impossible now.

THE GHOST OF DR JOSEPH BROWN

CHARLESTON
SOUTH CAROLINA

Dr. Joseph Brown was not a native of South Carolina; he was from Rhode Island, but had come South in the hope that warm weather would help improve his health. It was 1786, and Dr. Brown found himself in an inn that made him feel very uneasy. Still, he needed a place to spend the night and was preparing to book a room. He became increasingly scared as the men in the bar stared at him like he was a lamb and they were starving wolves. Suddenly, a gentleman, Ralph Isaacs, stepped into the inn and noticed Dr. Brown looked like a scared kitten. He told him that a gentleman like himself should not be staying in such a place and offered the doctor lodging in his home. Frightened, the doctor accepted the offer and quickly left the present company he was with. Both men were brought up to be gentlemen and had a lot in common; they became best friends in a very short time frame.

Dr. Brown built up a successful medical practice and soon found permanent accommodations with two elderly sisters at 59 Church, where there was a room to rent. The old women adored their new tenant; the thing they loved most about him was the way he came down the stairs with a spring in his step as he whistled a chipper tune. Ralph noticed that his pal was quickly growing in many of Charleston's social circles, even managing to surpass him in local standing. A vicious jealousy grew in Ralph and started to fester; the doctor's smallest comments or acts filled him with rage. Finally, one night he hit a boiling point. The friends had a disagreement over a performance in a play; the fight culminated in Ralph challenging Brown to a duel and, in a thoughtless moment of anger, Brown accepted the challenge.

As the duel started, Brown had cooled down and mistakenly assumed Ralph had as well. Brown fired his gun in the air to show his friend he wished him no harm, but sadly, Isaac did not have the same intentions. He did not want his former friend to just die, he wanted him to suffer. Ralph shot him in both knees, which left him on the ground in intense pain. Ralph was hoping that Brown would live the rest of his days as a cripple, but due to the inferior medical science at the time, the rest of his days was less than two weeks. His wounds became infected and poisoned his blood; he died in his bed at 59 Church Street.

Still, being shot and passing on has done nothing to dampen the good doctor's high spirits. Folks continue to hear him joyfully coming down the stairs, whistling a happy tune. He has become known as the Whistling Ghost of Charleston and has been heard for over two hundred years now. It is unlikely he will be leaving soon.

BRICK HOUSE RUINS

EDISTO ISLAND
SOUTH CAROLINA

The ghost of a murdered bride is rumored to haunt the shell of the old burned-down home on Edisto Island. The house was originally constructed in 1725 by a wealthy planter, Paul Hamilton. His massive home would stand for 204 years… until ultimately succumbing to a fire of unknown causes. Anyway, a bride was preparing for her big day and could not have been happier for her future. However, not everyone was thrilled with her decision. A suitor, rumored to be a man from Charleston, whom she had rejected countless times, was full of jealousy and rage. He saw her staring out the window as she wore her wedding dress. He snuck up as close as he could and shot through the glass. It struck her in the chest and she bled to death in a few minutes.

The tragedy scared the small community. She was laid to rest only a few days after she was meant to be wed. Shortly after the funeral, the home's residents started seeing the bride staring out the window she was shot from, with a small smile on her face. Others have claimed to see her walking the grounds, almost as if she is walking down the aisle. The house is not just a shell. No one has lived there for nearly a hundred years, but people still see the bride staring out the window, and occasionally they claim to hear her crying from the old home.

OLYMPIA MILLS

COLUMBIA
SOUTH CAROLINA

Olympia Mills, which was built in 1899, was one of the largest cotton mills in the United States. When it started for business, child labor laws did not exist and like most factories, the mill used children because their hands were small enough to have the ability to reach into equipment. Naturally, this had its share of problems, as many children lost limbs or died in the mill. In those days, all this would not even cause them to slow production down; the family was notified and the body was simply tossed somewhere like a sack of potatoes.

In 1996, the mill was shut down and sat vacant for years. It has recently been turned into apartments. People staying in these apartments have become convinced that the ghosts of those children still haunt the old mill. While taking a shower, small handprints appear on fogged-up mirrors, children's laughter is heard in empty hallways, and small kids are seen peeking around corners. It seems that because they spent their living years working like adults, they now spend their afterlife behaving like children.

BUBBA

COLUMBIA
SOUTH CAROLINA

It is now the state museum, but originally the huge structure was the Columbia Mills. It was constructed in 1893 and was used to produce textiles, which it did up until 1981, when it was shut down. The mill's owners did not want the building to go to waste, so they donated it to the state to be used how they wished. They turned it into the museum it is today. The place is full of visitors checking out the exhibits on display. There is so much to see that some people visit a couple days in a row, so they can take it all in. However, one guest has been there every day for the past two decades. Lovingly called Bubba, he is a man dressed in early 1900s overalls and boots and is seen walking through the building pretty often.

At first, some people mistake him for an actor the museum has hired. However, this viewpoint changes when he walks *through* a wall as onlookers watch. He is reported to be a friendly guy and very aware of his surroundings. He has been noticed checking out displays and reading signs on the wall, and even trying to use the elevator. Who he was in life is anyone's guess, as undoubtedly the old mill saw its share of death, just like most factories of the day. No matter for the people of the museum. He is not bitter or hostile about his passing as some spirits are...he just does not seem ready to go is all. So if you are in the museum and find yourself seeing Bubba, do not be scared — he is just appreciating the sights like you.

RICE MUSEUM

GEORGETOWN
SOUTH CAROLINA

It is hard to miss the Rice Museum, located on the bank of the Sampit River. This historic building sports a large tower complete with a historic clock. It is because of this it is also lovingly called the "Town Clock." Although it now serves as a museum, its original purpose, when constructed in 1842, was a market for the community. Everything from produce to slaves was sold there at its height. It has also served as a print shop, jail, and police station. The adjacent Kaminski building, constructed the same year as the market, was originally a retail space.

Both buildings are reportedly haunted, which is not hard to imagine with their long past. As for who and why, there is no definitive answer, although most think the majority of the ghosts are former slaves. It is believed that the spirit of an older slave woman is the most active entity in the building. One specter is heard walking the upstairs with what sounds to be a wooden leg; he is heard walking back and forth and up and downstairs. These spirits are heard whispering throughout the museums — it is never clear as to what they are saying.

The museum is always displaying wonderful pieces of the state's past, so it's possible because of this that these ghosts of the past feel at home there. The Town Clock is a must-see for anyone who loves history or the paranormal.

THE GHOST OF
THE CREDIT UNION

ANDERSON
SOUTH CAROLINA

I cannot leave Anderson without mentioning the ghost sighting that got national attention only a few years back. In June 2009, a security guard at Municipal Business Center noticed something on one of the monitors: a ball of light that seemed to have a mind of its own. He first thought it could be a robber's flashlight, so he went to inspect. However, he did not find anything at all, not even the odd light.

Over the next few nights, the light would show up on the monitor, always seeming to float around one particular chair in the room. Attempts were made to stop the light by making sure all the windows were covered and the guilty chair was moved to the other side of the room…yet, the light still appeared and followed the chair to its new location.

It became clear to most of the staff that this was not a trick of the light or some odd reflection. Nobody ever saw the light in person, but only caught it on the security camera. Also, no one reported any paranormal phenomenon in the building. It made some of the staff nervous, though. The video of the light went viral and showed up on countless news outlets tagged as the "Anderson Ghost."

People speculated on what it could be. Some tried to offer a scientific explanation, while others wanted to know whose ghost it was. Eventually, the ghostly light stopped showing up on the camera, which was fine with the employees.

The building seemed too new to be haunted, but during the 1890s, a carriage shop sat on the property. The carriage shop has no record of any tragedies ever occurring while in operation, although records from that era are far from complete. Ultimately, the phenomenon seemed to be more a one-time show than anything else. Whomever or whatever was responsible for the light has yet to return to the Credit Union.

RESOURCES

RESOURCES

www.americanfolkl ore.net/folklore/2011/07/the_
headless_sentry.html-1997 (2010)

www.angelfire.com/sc3/mytrip/alice.html (2004)

www.batterycarriagehouse.com/ghosts.html (2013)

www.charlestonuu.org/WhoWeAre/History/tabid/237/
Default.aspx (2007)

www.eatsleepplaybeaufort.
com/a-collection-of-beauforts-most-
haunted-tales (2012)

www.hauntedstories.net/myths-legends/south-
carolina/ghost-treasure-folly-island (2013)

www.litchfieldplantation.net/history

www.merridun.com/history.html (2010)

www.nps.gov/nr/travel/charleston/old.html (2012)

www.palmettodunes.com/blog/2011-10-14/
haunted-hilton-head-the-blue-lady-of-
palmetto-dunes (2011)

www.poogansporch.com/the-story/

www.sciway.net/hist/lands-end-light-st-helena-island.
html (2013)

www.technogypsie.com/faerie/?p=473. (2012)